Charles Knight

William Caxton, the first English Printer

A Biography

Charles Knight

William Caxton, the first English Printer
A Biography

ISBN/EAN: 9783337029258

Printed in Europe, USA, Canada, Australia, Japan

Cover: Foto ©Raphael Reischuk / pixelio.de

More available books at **www.hansebooks.com**

WILLIAM CAXTON,

THE FIRST ENGLISH PRINTER.

A Biography.

BY

CHARLES KNIGHT.

NEW EDITION.

LONDON:

WILLIAM CLOWES & SONS, | HARDWICKE & BOGUE,

13, CHARING CROSS, S.W. | 192, PICCADILLY, W.

1877.

NOTE.

———◆◇◆———

The re-issue of Charles Knight's "The Old Printer" has been considered appropriate to the celebration of the Quarcentenary of the Introduction of Printing into England. The author himself was a worthy follower of Caxton, and his name marks an era in the spread of literature by means of the printing press.

No alteration has been made in the text of the work; but since its original publication considerable advances, as the reader will notice, have been made towards the fulfilment of the author's aspirations.

All profits arising from the sale of this volume will be devoted to the "Caxton Fund" now being formed in connection with the Celebration of the Quarcentenary of the Introduction of Printing into England.

June, 1877.

CONTENTS.

LIST OF ILLUSTRATIONS.

WILLIAM CAXTON.

CHAPTER I.

N the first book printed in the English language, the subject of which was the 'Histories of Troy,' William Caxton, the translator of the work from the French, in his prologue or preface, says, by way of apology for his simpleness and imperfectness in the French and English languages, "In France was I never, and was born and learned mine English in Kent, in the Weald, where I doubt not is spoken as broad and rude English as in any place of England." The Weald of Kent is now a fertile district, rich in corn-land and pasture, with farm-houses and villages spread over its surface, intersected by good roads, and a railway running through the heart of it,

bringing the scattered inhabitants closer and closer to each other. But at the period when William Caxton was born, and learnt his English in the Weald, it was a wild district with a scanty population; its inhabitants had little intercourse with the towns, the affairs of the busy world went on without their knowledge and assistance, they were more separated from the great body of their countrymen than a settler in Canada or Australia is at the present day. It is easy to understand therefore why they should have spoken a " broad and rude English " at the time of Caxton's boyhood, during the reign of Henry V. and the beginning of that of Henry VI. William Lambarde, who wrote a hundred and fifty years after this period, having published his ' Perambulation of Kent' in 1570, mentions as a common opinion touching this Weald of Kent, " that it was a great while together in manner nothing else but a desert and waste wilderness, not planted with towns or peopled with men as the outsides of the shire were, but stored and stuffed with herds of deer and droves of hogs only ;" and he goes on to say that, " although the property of the Weald was at the first belonging to certain known owners, yet it was not then allotted into tenancies." The Weald of Kent came to be taken, he says, " even as men were contented to inhabit it, and by peacemeal to rid it of the wood, and to break it up with the plough." In some lonely farm, then, of this wild district, are we, upon the best of evidence, his own words, to fix the birth-place and the earliest home of the first English printer.

The father of William Caxton was in all probability a proprietor of land. At any rate, he desired to bestow upon his son all the advantages of education which that age could furnish. The honest printer, many years after his school-days, looks back upon that spring-time of his

life with feelings that make us honour the simple worth
of his character. In his 'Life of Charles the Great,'
printed in 1485, he says, " I have emprised [undertaken]
and concluded in myself to reduce [translate] this said
book into our English, as all along and plainly ye may
read, hear, and see, in this book here following. Beseeching all them that shall find fault in the same to correct
and amend it, and also to pardon me of the rude and
simple reducing. And though so be there no gay terms,
nor subtle nor new eloquence, yet I hope that it shall be
understood, and to that intent I have specially reduced it
after the simple cunning that God hath lent to me, whereof I humbly and with all my heart thank Him, and also
am bounden to pray for my father's and mother's souls,
that in my youth set me to school, by which, by the
sufferance of God, I get my living I hope truly. And
that I may so do and continue, I beseech Him to grant me
of His grace; and so to labour and occupy myself vir-
tuously, that I may come out of debt and deadly sin, that
after this life I may come to His bliss in heaven." Caxton
seems to have had the rare happiness to have had his
father about him to a late period of his life. According
to a record in the accounts of the churchwardens of the
parish church of St. Margaret's, Westminster, in which
parish the first printer carried on his business, it appears
that one William Caxton, who is conjectured to have been
the father, was buried on the 18th of May, 1480.

Some time before the period of Caxton's boyhood, a
great change had taken place in the general system of
education in England. In the time of Edward III., about
half a century before the period of which we speak, the
children in the grammar-schools were not taught English
at all. It was the policy of the first Norman kings, long
continued by their successors, to get rid of the old English

or Saxon language altogether; and to make the people
familiar with the Norman French, the language of the
conquerors. The new statutes of the realm were written
in French; so were the decisions of the judges, and the
commentaries on the laws in general. Ralph Higden, in
a sort of chronicle which Caxton printed, says, " Children
in schools, against the usage and manner of all other
nations, be compelled for to leave their own language,
and for to construe their lessons and . their things in
French; and so they have since Normans came first
into England. Also gentlemen be taught for to speak
French from the time that they rocked in their cradle,
and can speak and play with a child's brooch [stick
or other toy], and uplandishmen [countrymen] will
liken themselves to gentlemen, and delight with great
business for to speak French, to be told of." John de
Trevisa, the translator of Higden's 'Polychronicon,'
writing some forty years later, " This manner was much
used before the Great Plague, and is since some deal
changed; for Sir John Cornewaile, a master of grammar,
changed the teaching in grammar-schools, and construction in French; and other schoolmasters use the same way
now, in the year of our Lord 1385, the ninth year of
King Richard II., and leave all French in schools, and use
all construction in English. Wherein they have advantage one way:—that is, that they learn the sooner their
grammar; and in another, disadvantage, for now they
learn no French, which is hurt for them that shall pass
the sea." It was this change of system, operating upon
his early instruction, which caused Caxton, as a translator,
to be so diffident of his own capacity to render faithfully
what was before him out of French into English. Indeed
from his earliest youth to the close of his literary career,
the English language was constantly varying, through the

introduction of new words and phrases; and there was a
marked distinction between the courtly dialect and that of
the commonalty. We have seen how he speaks of the
broad and rude English of his native Weald. But towards
the close of his life, in a book printed by him in 1490, he
mentions the difficulty he had in pleasing "some gentlemen, which late blamed me, saying, that in my translations I had over curious terms, which could not be understood of common people, and desired me to use old and
homely terms in my translations. And fain would I
satisfy every man; and so to do, took an old book and
read therein; and certainly the English was so rude and
broad that I could not well understand it. And also my
Lord Abbot of Westminster did show to me late certain
evidences written in old English, for to reduce it into our
English now used, and certainly it was written in such
wise that it was more like to Dutch than English; I could
not reduce nor bring it to be understood. And certainly
our language now used varieth far from that which was
used and spoken when I was born: for we Englishmen be
born under the denomination of the moon, which is never
steadfast, but ever wavering, waxing one season, and
waneth and decreaseth another season; and that common
English that is spoken in one shire varieth from another.
Insomuch that in my days happened that certain merchants
were in a ship in Thames, for to have sailed over the sea
into Zealand, and for lack of wind they tarried at Fore-
land, and went to land for to refresh them; and one of
them named Sheffelde, a mercer, came into an house and
asked for meat, and especially he asked after *eggs;* and
the good wife answered, that she could speak no French;
and the merchant was angry, for he also could speak no
French, but would have had eggs, and she understood him
not. And then at last another said that he would have

eyren; then the good wife said that she understood him
well. Lo, what should a man in these days now write,
eggs or *eyren?* certainly it is hard to please every man, by
cause of diversity and change of language. For in these
days every man that is in any reputation in his country
will utter his communication and matters in such manners
and terms that few men shall understand them. And
some honest and good clerks have been with me, and
desired me to write the most curious terms that I could
find. And thus between plain, rude, and curious, I stand
abashed ; but in my judgment, the common terms that be
daily used be lighter [easier] to be understood than the old
and ancient English." In these days, when the same
language with very slight variations is spoken from one
end of the land to the other, it is difficult to imagine a
state of things such as Caxton describes, in which the
" common English which is spoken in one shire varieth
from another," and there was a marked distinction between
plain terms and curious terms. Easy and rapid communication, and above all the circulation of books, newspapers,
and other periodical works, all free from provincial expres-
sions, have made the " over curious terms which could not
be understood of common people " more familiar to them
than the "old and homely terms" which their forefathers
used in their several counties, according to the restricted
meanings which they retained in their local use. When
there were no books amongst the community in general,
there could be no universality of language. Of this want
of books we may properly exhibit some details, chiefly to
show one of the most remarkable differences which the
lapse of four centuries has produced in our country.

We shall find it, we think, a more agreeable, as well as
more instructive course, to look at the general subject of
the supply of books in connection with the orders of people

who were to use them, rather than presenting a number
of scattered facts, to exhibit the relative prices and scar ity
of books in what are called the middle ages. We will first
take the clergy, the scholars of those days. The mode in
which books were multiplied by transcribers in the monasteries is clearly described by Richard de Bury, bishop
of Durham, in his ' Philobiblon,' a treatise on the love of
books, written by him in Latin in 1344 :—" As it is necessary for a state to provide military arms, and prepare plentiful stores of provisions for soldiers who are about to fight, so
it is evidently worth the labour of the church militant to
fortify itself against the attacks of pagans and heretics
with a multitude of sound books. But because everything
that is serviceable to mortals suffers the waste of mortality
through lapse of time, it is necessary for volumes corroded
by age to be restored by renovated successors, that per-
petuity, repugnant to the nature of the individual, may be
conceded to the species. Hence it is that Ecclesiastes
significantly says, in the 12th chapter, ' There is no end
of making many books.' For as the bodies of books suffer
continual detriment from a combined mixture of con-
traries in their composition, so a remedy is found out by
the prudence of clerks, by which a holy book paying the
debt of nature may obtain an hereditary substitute, and a
seed may be raised up like to the most holy deceased, and
that saying of Ecclesiasticus, chapter 30, be verified, ' The
father is dead, and as it were not dead, for he hath left
behind him a son like unto himself.' " The invention of
paper, about a century and a half before Richard de Bury
wrote, and its general employment instead of vellum for
manuscripts in ordinary use, was a great step towards
the multiplication of books. Transcribers necessarily
became more numerous; but for a long period they wholly
belonged to the monastic orders, and the books were

c

essentially for the use of the clergy. Richard de Bury
says, with the most supreme contempt for all others, whatever be their rank, "Laymen, to whom it matters not
whether they look at a book turned wrong side upwards
or spread before them in its natural order, are altogether
unworthy of any communion with books." But even to
the privileged classes he is not sparing of his reproach as
to the misuse of books. He reprobates the unwashed
hands, the dirty nails, the greasy elbows leaning upon
the volume, the munching of fruit and cheese over the
open leaves, which were the marks of careless and idle
readers. With a solemn reverence for a book at which
we may smile, but with a smile of respect, he says, "Let
there be a mature decorum in opening and closing of
volumes, that they may neither be unclasped with
precipitous haste, nor thrown aside after inspection without being duly closed." The good bishop bestowed
certain portions of his valuable library upon a company
of scholars residing in a Hall at Oxford; and one of his
chapters is entitled ' A provident arrangement by which
books may be lent to strangers,' meaning, by strangers,
students of Oxford not belonging to that Hall. One of
these arrangements is as follows :—" Five of the scholars
dwelling in the aforesaid Hall are to be appointed by the
master of the same Hall, to whom the custody of the
books is to be deputed. Of which five, three, and in no
case fewer, shall be competent to lend any books for
inspection and use only ; but for copying and transcribing
we will not allow any book to pass without the walls of
the house. Therefore, when any scholar, whether secular
or religious, whom we have deemed qualified for the
present favour, shall demand the loan of a book, the
keepers must carefully consider whether they have a
duplicate of that book ; and if so, they may lend it to him,

taking a security which in their opinion shall exceed in value the book delivered." Anthony Wood, who in the seventeenth century wrote the lives of eminent Oxford men, speaks of this library which was given to Durham College (now Trinity College) as containing more books than all the bishops of England had then in their custody. He adds, "After they had been received they were for many years kept in chests, under the custody of several scholars deputed for that purpose." In the time of Henry IV. a library was built in that college, and then, says Wood, "the said books were put into pews, or studies, and chained to them." The statutes of St. Mary's College, Oxford, in the reign of Henry VI., are quoted by Warton, in his 'History of English Poetry,' as furnishing a remarkable instance of the inconveniences and impediments to study which must have been produced by a scarcity of books: "Let no scholar occupy a book in the library above one hour, or two hours at most, so that others shall be hindered from the use of the same." This certainly shows the scarcity of books; but not such a scarcity as at an early period of the Church, when one book was given out by the librarian to each of a religious fraternity at the beginning of Lent, to be read diligently during the year, and to be returned the following Lent. The original practice of keeping the books in chests would seem to indicate that they could not be very frequently changed by the readers; and the subsequent plan of chaining them to the desks gives the notion that, like many other things tempting by their rarity, they could not be safely trusted in the hands of those who might rather covet the possession than the use. It was a very common thing to write in the first leaf of a book, " Cursed be he who shall steal or tear out the leaves, or in any way injure this book."

c 2

We have abundant evidence, whatever be the scarcity of books as compared with the growth of scholarship, that the ecclesiastics laboured most diligently to multiply books for their own establishments. In every great abbey there was a room called the Scriptorium, where boys and novices were constantly employed in multiplying the service-books of the choir, and the less valuable books for the library; whilst the monks themselves laboured in their cells upon bibles and missals. Equal pains were taken in providing books for those who received a liberal education

Transcriber at Work.

in collegiate establishments. Warton says, " At the foundation of Winchester College, one or more transcribers were hired and employed by the founder to make books for the library. They transcribed and took their commons within the college, as appears by computations of expenses on their account now remaining." But there are several indications that even kings and nobles had not the advantages of scholars by profession; and, possessing few books of their own, had sometimes to borrow of their more favoured subjects. We find it recorded that the Prior of Christ Church, Canterbury, had lent to King Henry V.

the works of St. Gregory, and he complains that after the
king's death the book had been detained by the Prior of
Shene. The same king had borrowed from the Lady West-
moreland two books that had not been returned, and a petition is still extant in which she begs his successors in
authority to let her have them back again. Lewis XI. of
France wishing to borrow a book from the Faculty of
Medicine at Paris, they would not allow the king to have it
till he had deposited a quantity of valuable plate in pledge,
and given a joint bond with one of his nobles for its due
return. The books that were to be found in the palaces
of the great, a little while before the invention of printing, were for the most part highly illuminated manuscripts, and bound in the most expensive style. In the
wardrobe accounts of King Edward IV. we find that Piers
Bauduyn is paid for "binding, gilding, and dressing" of
two books, twenty shillings each, and of four books,
sixteen shillings each. Now twenty shillings in those
days would have bought an ox. But the cost of this
binding and garnishing does not stop here; for there
were delivered to the binder six yards of velvet, six yards
of silk, laces, tassels, copper and gilt clasps, and gilt nails.
The price of velvet and silk in those days was enormous.
We may reasonably conclude that these royal books were as
much for show as for use. One of the books thus garnished
by Edward IV.'s binder is called 'Le Bible Historiaux'
(The Historical Bible), and there are several copies of the
same book in manuscript in the British Museum. In one
of them the following paragraph is written in French:
" This book was taken from the King of France at the
battle of Poitiers; and the good Count of Salisbury,
William Mountague, bought it for a hundred marks, and
gave it to his lady Elizabeth, the good Countess. . . . . .
Which book the said Countess assigned to her executors

to sell for forty livres." We learn from another source that the great not only procured books by purchase, but employed transcribers to make them for their libraries. We find, from the manuscript account of the expenses of Sir John Howard, afterwards Duke of Norfolk, that in 1467 Thomas Lympnor, that is, Thomas the Limner, of Bury, was paid the sum of fifty shillings and twopence for a book which he had transcribed and ornamented, including the vellum and binding. The Limner's bill is made up of a number of items,—for whole vignettes, and half vignettes, and capital letters, and flourishing, and plain writing. This curious account is printed in the 'Paston Letters.' A letter of Sir John Paston, who is writing to his mother in 1474, shows how scarce money was in those days for the purchase of luxuries like books. He says, " As for the books that were Sir James's (the Priest's), if it like you that I may have them, I am not able to buy them, but somewhat would I give, and the remainder, with a good devout heart, by my troth, I will pray for his soul. . . . . . If any of them are claimed hereafter, in faith I will restore it." The custom of borrowing books and not returning them was as old, we see, as the days of the Red and White Roses. John Paston left an inventory of his books, eleven in number, although some of the eleven contained various little tracts bound together. One of the items in this catalogue is, " A Book of Troilus, which William B—— hath had near ten years, and lent it to Dame Wingfeld, and there I saw it."

But, even in the days before printing, there was a small book-trade; and schemes were devised for making books of some general use. In Paris, in the middle of the 14th century, the booksellers were commanded to keep books for hire; and, in a register of the University of Paris, Chevillier found a list of the books so circulated, and the

price of reading each.   The hire of a Bible was ten sous.
That the ecclesiastics and lawyers constituted the great
bulk of readers, and that the addition of a book, even to
the private library of a student, was a rare occurrence, is
evident from the absolute necessity for manuscript books
being dear.   If the number of readers had increased—if
there had been more candidates for the learned professions
—if the nobility had discovered the shame of their
ignorance—if learning had made its way to the franklin's
hall—manuscript books could never have been cheap.
But from the hour when a first large expense of trans-
ferring the letters, syllables, words, and sentences of a
manuscript to movable type was ascertained to be the
means of multiplying copies to the extent of any demand,
then the greater the demand the greater the cheapness.

If the nobles, the higher gentry, and even the lawyers
and ecclesiastics, were indifferently provided with books,
we cannot expect that the yeomen had any books whatever.   The merchants and citizens were probably somewhat better provided.   The labourers, who were scarcely
yet fully established in their freedom from bondage to one
lord, were probably, as a class, wholly unable to use
books at all.   Shakspere, in all likelihood, did not much
exaggerate the feelings of ignorant men, who at the same
time were oppressed men, when he puts these words in
the mouth of Jack Cade when addressing Lord Say:
" Thou hast most traitorously corrupted the youth of the
realm, in erecting a grammar-school: and whereas, before,
our forefathers had no other books but the score and the
tally, thou hast caused printing to be used; and, contrary
to the king, his crown and dignity, thou hast built a
paper-mill."   The poet has a little deranged the exact
order of events, as poets are justified in doing, who look
at history not with chronological accuracy, but with a

broad view of the connection between events and principles. The insurrection of Cade preceded the introduction
of printing and paper-mills into England. Although
during four centuries we have yet to lament that the
people have not had the full benefit which the art of
printing is calculated to bestow upon them, we may be
sure that during its progress the general amelioration of
society has been certain, though gradual. There can no
longer be any necessary exclusiveness in the possession
of books, and in the advantages which the knowledge of
books is calculated to bestow on all men. The late
Mr. Southey, a just and liberal thinker, but, like many
others of ardent feelings, sometimes mistaken and oftener
misrepresented, has truly pointed out the difference between the state of society when William Caxton was
raised up to do his work amongst us and the present
state. The following is an extract from his 'Colloquies
on the Progress and Prospects of Society:' "One of the
first effects of printing was to make proud men look upon
learning as disgraced, by being thus brought within
reach of the common people. Till that time learning,
such as it was, had been confined to courts and convents,
the low birth of the clergy being overlooked, because
they were privileged by their order. But when laymen
in humble life were enabled to procure books, the pride
of aristocracy took an absurd course, insomuch that at
one time it was deemed derogatory for a nobleman if he
could read or write. Even scholars themselves complained
that the reputation of learning, and the respect due to it,
and its rewards, were lowered when it was thrown open
to all men : and it was seriously proposed to prohibit the
printing of any book that could be afforded for sale below
the price of three soldi. This base and invidious feeling
was perhaps never so directly avowed in other countries

as in Italy, the land where literature was first restored; and yet in this more liberal island ignorance was for some generations considered to be a mark of distinction by which a man of gentle birth chose, not unfrequently, to make it apparent that he was no more obliged to live by the toil of his brain than by the sweat of his brow. The same changes in society, which rendered it no longer possible for this class of men to pass their lives in idleness, have completely put an end to this barbarous pride. It is as obsolete as the fashion of long finger-nails, which in some parts of the East are still the distinctive mark of those who labour not with their hands. All classes are now brought within the reach of your current literature,— that literature which, like a moral atmosphere, is, as it were, the medium of intellectual life, and on the quality of which, according as it may be salubrious or noxious, the health of the public mind depends."

CHAPTER II.

N a book which Caxton printed in 1483, 'The
Booke callyd Cathon,' he says in his prologue
or preface, " Unto the noble, ancient, and renowned city, the city of London in England,
I, William Caxton, citizen and conjury [sworn
fellow] of the same, and of the fraternity and fellowship
of the Mercery, owe of right my service and good will;
and of very duty am bounden naturally to assist, aid,
and counsel, as farforth as I can to my power, as to my
mother of whom I have received my nurture and living;
and shall pray for the good prosperity and policy of the

same during my life. For as me seemeth it is of great
need, by cause I have known it in my young age much
more wealthy, prosperous, and richer than it is at this
day ; and the cause is, that there is almost none that
intendeth to the common weal, but only every man for
his singular profit." It is the usual habit of the aged to
look back upon the days of their youth as a period of
higher prosperity and more exalted virtue, public and
private, than they witness in their declining years. This
is in most cases merely the mind's own colouring of the
picture. But it is very possible that London, in the first
year of Richard III., when Caxton wrote this preface, was
really less prosperous, and its citizens less devoted to the
public good, than half a century earlier, when Caxton
was a blithe apprentice within its walls. The country
had passed through the terrible convulsion of the wars of
the Roses ; and it is the nature of civil wars, especially,
not only to waste the substance and destroy the means
of existence of every man, but to render all men selfish,
grasping at temporary good, suspicious, faithless. The
master of Caxton was Robert Large, a member of the
Mercers' Company, who was one of the Sheriffs in 1430,
and Lord Mayor in 1439–40. The date of Caxton's ap-
prenticeship has not been ascertained ; but it is considered
by several of his biographers to have commenced about
1428. At this period, the sixth of Henry VI., a law was
on the statute-book, and rigorously enforced, whose object
was to prevent the sons of labourers in husbandry, and
indeed of the poorer classes of the yeomanry, from rising
out of the condition in which they were born, by partici-
pating in the higher gains of trade and handicraft. A
law of the seventh of Henry IV., about two-and-twenty
years before this conjectural period of Caxton's apprentice-
ship, recites that, according to ancient statutes, those who

labour at the plough or cart, or other service of husbandry,
till at the age of twelve years, should continue to abide
at such labour, and not to be put to any mystery or
handicraft;—notwithstanding which statutes, says the
law of Henry IV., country people whose fathers and
mothers have no land or rent are put apprentices to divers
crafts within the cities and boroughs, so that there is
great scarcity of labourers and other servants of husbandry. The law then declares, "That no man nor
woman, of what estate or condition they be, shall put
their son or daughter, of whatsoever age he or she be, to
serve as apprentice to no craft or other labour within any
city or borough in the realm, except he have land or rent
to the value of twenty shillings by the year at least, but
they shall be put to other labours as their estates doth
require, upon pain of one year's imprisonment." This
iniquitous law was necessarily as demoralizing and as
injurious to the national prosperity as the institution of
castes in India. Yet, by a most extraordinary blindness
to cause and consequence, the makers of the law provided
in the most direct way for its overthrow; for the statute
goes on to say, that, although the husbandry labourer is
always to be a labourer, "every man or woman, of what
estate or condition they be, shall be free to set their son
or daughter to take learning at any manner school that
pleaseth them within the realm." The citizens of London,
much to their honour, procured a repeal of this act in the
eighth of Henry VI., about the period when Caxton was
apprenticed. The probability is, that he would not have
been affected by the exclusive character of this law;
for his master was a rich and distinguished mercer—a
member of that association which has always had pre-
eminence amongst the livery companies of London. The
dignified gravity, the prudence, and the prosperity of

the citizens of that day have been well described by
Chaucer :—

> "A Merchant was there with a forkéd beard;
> In motley, and high on horse he sat,
> And on his head a Flaundrish beaver hat.
> His bootés claspéd fair and fetisly; *
> His reasons spake he full solemncly,
> Sounding alway the increase of his winning:
> He would the sea were kept † for any thing,
> Betwixen Middleburgh and Oréwell.
> Well could he in exchanges shieldiés ‡ sell,
> This worthy man full well his wit beset; §
> There wisté no wight that he was in debt,
> So stedfastly did he his governance
> With his bargains, and with his chevisance." ‖

When we look at William Caxton as the apprentice
to a London mercer, his position does not at first sight
appear very favourable to that cultivation of a literary
taste, and that love of books, which was originally the
solace, and afterwards the business, of his life.   Yet a
closer insight into the mercantile arrangements of those
days will show us that he could not have been more
favourably placed for attaining some practical acquaintance with books, in the way of his ordinary occupation.
When books were so costly and so inaccessible to the
great body of the people, there was necessarily no special
trade of bookselling.   There were indeed stationers, who
had books for sale, or more probably executed orders for
transcribing books.   Their occupation is thus described
by Mr. Hallam, in his 'Literature of Europe :'—" These
dealers were denominated stationarii, perhaps from the
open stalls at which they carried on their business, though

* Neatly.   † Guarded.
‡ French crowns, which were stamped with a shield.
§ Employed.   ‖ An agreement for borrowing money.

statio is a general word for a shop, in low Latin. They
appear by the old statutes of the university of Paris,
and by those of Bologna, to have sold books upon commission; and are sometimes, though not uniformly, distinguished from the librarii; a word which, having
originally been confined to the copyists of books, was
afterwards applied to those who traded in them. They
sold parchment and other materials of writing, which,
with us, though, as far as I know, nowhere else, have
retained the name of stationery, and naturally exercised the kindred occupations of binding and decorating.
They probably employed transcribers." The mercer in
those days was not a dealer in small wares generally,
as at an earlier period; nor was his trade confined
to silken goods—such an one as Shakspere describes,
"Master Threepile, the mercer," who had thrown a man
into prison for "some four suits of peach-coloured satin."
The mercer of the fifteenth century was essentially a
merchant. The mercers in the time of Edward III. were
the great wool-dealers of the country. They were the
merchants of the Staple, in the early days of our woollen
manufacture; and the merchant adventurers of a later
period were principally of their body. (In their traffic
with other lands, and especially with the Low Countries,
they were the agents by which valuable manuscripts
found their way into England; and in this respect they
were something like the great merchant princes of Italy,
whose ships not unfrequently contained a cargo of Indian
spices and of Greek manuscripts. John Bagford, who
wrote a slight Life of Caxton about 1714, which is in
manuscript in the British Museum, says, "Kings, queens,
and noblemen had their particular merchants, who, when
they were ready for their voyage into foreign parts, sent
their servants to know what they wanted, and among the

rest of their choice many times books were demanded, and there to buy them in those parts where they were going." Caxton tells us in the 'Book of Good Manners,' which he translated from the French and printed in 1487, that the original French work was delivered to him by a "special friend, a mercer of London, named William Praat." This commerce of books could not have been very great; but it might have been so far carried on by Robert Large, the wealthy master of Caxton, that a lad of ability might thus possess opportunities for improvement which were denied to the great body of his fellow-apprentices. At this particular period there appear to have been but few opportunities even for the sons of parents of some substance to obtain the rudiments of knowledge. There is a petition presented to Parliament in the twenty-fifth year of Henry VI., 1446, which exhorts the Commons " to con- sider the great number of grammar-schools that sometime were in divers parts of this realm, besides those that were in London, and how few there are in these days." The petitioners, who are four clergymen of the city, go on to say that London is the common concourse of this land, and that many persons, for lack of schoolmasters in their own country, resort there to be informed of grammar; and then they proceed thus: "Wherefore it were expe- dient that in London were a sufficient number of schools and good informers in grammar; and not, for the singular avail of two or three persons, grievously to hurt the mul- titude of young people of all this land. For where there is great number of learners and few teachers, and all the learners be compelled to go to the few teachers, and to none others, the masters wax rich of money, and the learners poorer in cunning, as experience openly showeth, against all virtue and order of weal public." These benevolent clergymen accomplished the object of their

petition, which was that in each of their parishes they
might "ordain, create, establish, and set a person sufficiently learned in grammar to hold and exercise a school
in the same science of grammar, and there to teach to all
that will learn." One of the schools thus established
exists to this day, in connection with the Mercers' Company, and is commonly known as the Mercers' School.
We are a little anticipating the period of our narrative,
for this petition belongs to Caxton's mature life; but we
mention it as an evidence of the extreme difficulty which
must have existed in those days for the children of the
middle classes to obtain the rudiments of knowledge. It
is evident that Caxton belonged to the more fortunate
portion, upon whom the blessings of education fell like
prizes in a lottery. The evil has not been wholly corrected even during four centuries; but it is devoutly to
be hoped that the time is not far distant when, to use the
words of the benevolent clergymen who knew the value
of knowledge at that comparatively dark period, there
shall be in every place a school, and a competent person
"there to teach to all that will learn."

Oldys, the writer of the Life of Caxton in the 'Biographia Britannica,' says, speaking of Robert Large, the
master of Caxton, "The same magistrate held his mayor-
alty in that which had been the mansion-house of Robert
Fitzwalter, anciently called the Jews' Synagogue, at the
north corner of the Old Jewry." This Old Jewry appears
to have been in earlier times an accustomed place of residence for the mercers; for there are records still extant of
legal proceedings in the time of Henry III. against four
mercers of that place, for a violent assault upon two
Lombard merchants, whom they regarded as rivals in trade.
In the days of their retail dealings they occupied a portion
of Cheapside which went by the name of the Mercery.

In the fourteenth century their shops were little better than sheds, and Cheapside, or more properly Cheap, was a sort of market, where various trades collected round the old Cross, which remained there till the time of the Long Parliament. When the mercers became large wholesale dealers in woollen cloths and silk, the haberdashers took up their standing in the same place. In the ballad of 'London Lickpenny,' written in the time of Henry VI., the scene in the Cheap is thus described:—

> "Then to the Cheap I began me drawn,
>   Where much people I saw for to stand;
> One offered me velvet, silk, and lawn,
>   Another he taketh me by the hand,
> 'Here is Paris thread, the finest in the land.'"

The city apprentice in the days of Caxton was a staid sober youth, who, although of gentle blood (as the regulations for the admittance of freemen required him to be), was meanly clothed, and subjected to the performance of even household drudgery. We learn from a tract called the 'City's Advocate,' printed in · 1628, that the ancient habit of the apprentices was a flat round cap, hair close cut, narrow falling bands, coarse side-coats (long coats), close hose, close stockings, and other such severe apparel. They walked before their masters and mistresses at night, bearing a lantern, and wearing a long club on their necks. But the mercer's apprentice had some exceptions which set him above his fellows : "Anciently it was the general use and custom of all apprentices in London (mercers only excepted, being commonly merchants and a better rank as it seems) to carry water-tankards to serve their masters' houses with water fetched either from the Thames or the common conduits." But, with all his restraints, the city apprentice was ever prone to frolic, and too often to mischief. The apprentices were a formidable body in the

D

days of the Tudors, sometimes defying the laws, and raising
tumults which have more than once ended in the prison and
the halter. Chaucer, writing some few years before the
term of Caxton's service, describes the love of sight-seeing
which was characteristic of the London apprentice :—

> "When there any ridings were in Cheap,
> Out of the shop thither would he leap;
> And till that he had all the sight yseen,
> And danced well, he would not come again."

Cheap was the great highway of processions; and London
was the constant theatre of triumphs and pageants, by
which the wealthy citizens expressed their devotion to
their ruling authorities. In the fifteenth century, when
the very insecurity of the tenure of the crown demanded
a more ardent display of public opinion, the London
apprentice had " ridings " enough to look upon, where the
pageantry was a real expression of power and magnificence,
and not a tawdry mockery, as that which now disgraces
the city of London once a year. Froissart describes the
riding of Henry IV. to his coronation. The entry of his
illustrious son into London after the battle of Agincourt
was another of these remarkable ridings. This, which was
an occasion of real enthusiasm, took place in Caxton's
childhood. But in 1432, when he is held to have been an
apprentice, the boy king, Henry VI., upon his return from
being crowned King of France, entered London with a
magnificence which chroniclers and poets have vied in
recording. Robert Fabyan, an alderman of London, who
wrote in the reign of Henry VII., describes this ceremonial
with such an admiration of the pomp as only one could be
supposed to feel who was born, as Chaucer says,

> "To sitten in a guildhall on the dais."

To look forward to such occasions of pomp was a satisfaction to the people, who knew nothing of the real workings

of public affairs, and saw only the outward indications of
success or misfortune. The reign of Henry VI. was an
unhappy one for the citizens of London. Violent contests
for authority, insurrections, battles for the crown, left their
fearful traces upon the course of the next thirty years.
But during Caxton's boyhood the evil days seemed distant.

In the books of the Brewers' Company, which, like all
other records, were for the most part in Norman French,
there is a curious entry in the reign of Henry V., which
records a great change in the habits of the people. The
entry is in Latin, and is thus translated : " Whereas our
mother-tongue, to wit, the English language, hath in
modern days begun to be honourably enlarged and adorned,
for that our most excellent lord King Henry the Fifth,
hath in his letters missive, and divers affairs touching his
own person, more willingly chosen to declare the secrets
of his will ; and for the better understanding of his people
hath, with a diligent mind, procured the common idiom
(setting aside others) to be commended by the exercise of
writing ; and there are many of our craft of brewers who
have the knowledge of writing and reading in the said
English idiom, but in others, to wit, the Latin and French,
before these times used, they do not in any wise understand ; for which causes, with many others, it being considered how that the greater part of the lords and trusty
commons have begun to make their matters to be noted
down in our mother-tongue, so we also in our craft, following in some manner their steps, have decreed in future to
commit to memory the needful things which concern us, as
appeareth in the following."

The assertion of the Brewers' Company, in the reign of
Henry V., that " the English language hath in modern
days begun to be honourably enlarged and adorned,"
rested, we apprehend, upon broader foundations than the

"letters missive" of the king in the common idiom. Great writers had arisen in our native tongue, with whose productions the nobler and wealthier classes at any rate were familiar. The very greatest of these, —the greatest name even now in our literature, with one exception,—must have furnished employment to hundreds of transcribers. The poems of Geoffrey Chaucer were familiar to all well-educated men, however scanty was the supply of copies and dear their cost. That Caxton himself was acquainted in his youth with these great works we cannot have a doubt. When it became his fortunate lot to multiply editions of the Canterbury Tales, and to render them accessible to a much larger class of the people than in the days when he himself first knew the solace and the delight of literature, he applied himself to the task with all the earnestness of an early love. In his preface to the second edition of the Canterbury Tales he thus delivers himself, with more than common enthusiasm : " Great thanks, laud, and honour ought to be given unto the clerks, poets, and historiographs that have written many noble books of wisdom of the lives, passions, and miracles of holy saints, of histories, of noble and famous acts and faits [deeds], and of the chronicles sith [since] the beginning of the creation of the world unto this present time ; by which we are daily informed and have knowledge of many things, of whom we should not have known if they had not left to us their monuments written. Amongst whom, and in especial before all other, we ought to give a singular laud unto that noble and great philosopher Geoffrey Chaucer, the which, for his ornate writing in our tongue, may well have the name of a laureat poet. For before that he, by his labour, embellished, ornated, and made fair our English, in this royaume [kingdom] was had rude speech and incongrue [incongruous], as yet it appeareth by old books, which at this day ought not to have place nor be compared among nor to his beauteous volumes and ornate writings, of whom he made many books and treatises of many a noble history, as well in metre as in rhyme and prose; and them so craftily made, that he comprehended his matters in short, quick, and high sentences; eschewing prolixity, casting away the chaff of superfluity, and shewing the picked grain of sentence, uttered by crafty and sugared eloquence." Again, in his edition of Chaucer's 'Book of Fame' he says, "Which work, as me seemeth, is craftily made, and worthy to be written and known: for he toucheth in it right great wisdom and subtle understanding; and so in all his works he excelleth in mine opinion all other writers in our English; for he writeth no void words, but all his matter is full of high and quick sentence, to whom ought to be given land and praising for his noble making and writing. For of him all other have borrowed sith, and taken in all their well saying and writing." There is another passage in the second edition of the Canterbury Tales which we quote here, not for the purpose of showing Caxton's honourable character as a printer, for that belongs to a subsequent period, but to point out that manuscripts of Chaucer were in private hands, varying indeed in their text, as books must have varied that were produced by different transcribers, but still keeping up the fame of the poet, and highly valued by their possessors: "Of which book so incorrect was one brought to me six year passed, which I supposed had been very true and correct, and according to the same I did imprint a certain number of them, which anon were sold to many and divers gentlemen: of whom one gentleman came to me, and said that this book was not according in many places unto the book that Geoffrey Chaucer had made. To whom I answered, that I had made it according to my copy, and by me was

nothing added nor diminished. Then he said he knew a
book which his father had and much loved, that was very
true, and according unto his own first book by him made;
and said more, if I would imprint it again, he would get
me the same book for a copy. How be it, he wist well
his father would not gladly part from it; to whom I said,
in case that he could get me such a book true and correct,
that I would once endeavour me to imprint it again, for
to satisfy the author: whereas before by ignorance I erred
in hurting and defaming his book in divers places, in
setting in some things that he never said nor made, and
leaving out many things that he made which are requisite
to be set in. And thus we fell at accord; and he full
gently got me of his father the said book, and delivered
it to me, by which I have corrected my book."

There was another poet of considerable popularity who
was contemporary with Chaucer. With the works of
Gower, Caxton must have been familiar. His principal
poem, 'Confessio Amantis,' was printed by Caxton in 1483,
and is said to have been the most extensively circulated of
all the books that came from his press. The poem is full of
stories that were probably common to all Europe, running
on through thousands of lines with wonderful fluency,
but little force. He was called the "moral Gower" by
Chaucer. The play of Pericles, ascribed to Shakspere, is
founded upon one of these stories. Gower himself shows
us what was the general course of reading in those days:—

> "Full oft time it falleth so,
> Mine ear with a good pittance
> Is fed of reading of romance,
> Of Idoyne, and of Amadas,
> That whilom * weren † in my case,
> And eke of other many a score,
> That loveden ‡ long ere I was bore." §

---

* Formerly.   † Were.   ‡ Loved.   § Born.

The romances of chivalry, the stories of " fierce wars and
faithful loves," were especially the delight of the great
and powerful. When the noble was in camp, he solaced
his hours of leisure with the marvellous histories of King
Arthur or Launcelot of the Lake ; and when at home, he
listened to or read the same stories in the intervals of the
chase or the feast. Froissart tells in his own simple and
graphic manner how he presented a book to King Richard
the Second, and how the king delighted in the subject of
the book : " Then the king desired to see my book that
I had brought for him ; so he saw it in his chamber, for
I had laid it there ready on his bed. When the king
opened it, it pleased him well, for it was fair illumined
and written, and covered with crimson velvet, with ten
buttons of silver and gilt, and roses of gold in the midst,
with two great clasps, gilt, richly wrought. Then the
king demanded me whereof it treated, and I showed him
how it treated matters of love, whereof the king was glad,
and looked in it, and read it in many places, for he could
speak and read French very well." Froissart was a
Frenchman and wrote in French ; but even Englishmen
wrote in French at that period, and some of Gower's early
poems are in French. According to his own account, the
long poem of the ' Confessio Amantis,' which was written
in English, was executed at the command of the same
King Richard :—

> " He hath this charge upon me laid,
> And bad me do my business,
> That to his high worthiness
> Some new thing I should book,
> That he himself it might look,
> After the form of my writing."

Chaucer and Gower lived some time before the period
of Caxton's youth in London. But there was a poet very

popular in his day, whom he can scarcely have avoided
having seen playing a conspicuous part in the high city
festivals. This was John Lydgate, monk of Bury, who
thus describes himself:

> "I am a monk by my profession,
>   Of Bury, called John Lydgate by my name,
> And wear a habit of perfection,
>   Although my life agree not with the same."

Thomas Warton has thus exhibited the nature of his
genius: "No poet seems to have possessed a greater
versatility of talents. He moves with equal ease in every
mode of composition. His hymns and his ballads have
the same degree of merit: and whether his subject be the
life of a hermit or a hero, of Saint Austin or Guy Earl of
Warwick, ludicrous or legendary, religious or romantic, a
history or an allegory, he writes with facility. His tran-
sitions were rapid from works of the most serious and
laborious kind to sallies of levity and pieces of popular
entertainment. His muse was of universal access, and he
was not only the poet of his monastery, but of the world
in general. If a disguising was intended by the company
of goldsmiths, a mask before his majesty at Eltham, a May
game for the sheriffs and aldermen of London, a mumming
before the lord mayor, a procession of pageants from the
creation for the festival of Corpus Christi, or a carol for a
coronation, Lydgate was consulted and gave the poetry."
A fine illuminated drawing in one of Lydgate's manuscripts, now in the British Museum, represents him presenting a book to the Earl of Salisbury. Such a presen-
tation may be regarded as the first publication of a new
work. The royal or noble person at whose command it
was written bestowed some rich gift upon the author,
which would be his sole pecuniary recompense, unless he
received some advantage from the transcribers, for the

copies which they multiplied. Doubtful as the rewards
of authorship may be when the multiplication of copies by
the press enables each reader to contribute a small acknow-
ledgment of the benefit which he receives, the literary
condition must have been far worse when the poet, humbly
kneeling before some mighty man, as Lydgate does in the

Lydgate presenting a book to the Earl of Salisbury.

picture, might have been dismissed with contumely, or
his present received with a low appreciation of the labour
and the knowledge required to produce it. The fame,
however, of a popular writer reached his ears in a far
more direct and flattering manner than belongs to the
literary honours of modern days. There can be little

doubt that the narrative poems of Chaucer and Gower
and Lydgate were familiar to the people through the
recitations of the minstrels. An agreeable writer on the
Rise and Progress of English Poetry, Mr. George Ellis,
says, " Chaucer, in his address to his Troilus and Cressida,
tells us it was intended to be read ' or elles sung,' which
must relate to the chanting recitation of the minstrels,
and a considerable part of our old poetry is simply
addressed to an audience, without any mention of readers.
That our English minstrels at any time united all the
talents of the profession, and were at once poets and
reciters and musicians, is extremely doubtful; but that
they excited and directed the efforts of their contemporary
poets to a particular species of composition, is as evident
as that a body of actors must influence the exertions of
theatrical writers. They were, at a time when reading
and writing were rare accomplishments, the principal
medium of communication between authors and the
public; and their memory in some measure supplied
the deficiency of manuscripts, and probably preserved
much of our early literature till the invention of printing." We may thus learn, that, although the number
of those was very few whose minds by reading could be
lifted out of the grovelling thoughts and petty cares of
every-day life, yet that the compositions of learned and
accomplished men, who still hold a high rank in our
literature, might be familiar to the people through the
agency of a numerous body of singers or reciters. There
has been a good deal of controversy about the exact
definition of the minstrel character—whether the minstrels were themselves poets and romance-writers, or the
depositaries of the writings of others and of the tra-
ditional literature of past generations. Ritson, a writer
upon this subject, says, " that there were individuals

formerly who made it their business to wander up and down the country chanting romances, and singing songs and ballads to the harp, fiddle, or more humble and less artificial instruments, cannot be doubted." They were a very numerous body a century before Chaucer; and most indefatigable in the prosecution of their trade. There is a writ or declaration of Edward the Second, which recites the evil of idle persons, under colour of minstrelsy, being received in other men's houses to meat and drink; and then goes on to direct that to the houses of great people no more than three or four minstrels of honour should come at the most in one day, "and to the houses of meaner men that none come unless he be desired, and such as shall come to hold themselves contented with meat and drink, and with such courtesy as the master of the house will show unto them of his own goodwill, without their asking of anything." Nothing can more clearly exhibit the general demand for the services of this body of men; for the very regulation as to the nature of their reward shows clearly that they were accustomed to require liberal payment, approaching perhaps to extortion; and then comes in the State to say that they shall not have a free market for their labour. They struggled on, sometimes prosperous and sometimes depressed, according to the condition of the country, till the invention of printing came to make popular literature always present in a man's house. The *book* of ballads or romances, which was then to be bought, was contented to abide there without any "meat and drink." In the words of Richard de Bury, whom we quoted in the first chapter, books "are the masters who instruct us without rods, without hard words and anger, without clothes and money. If you approach them, they are not asleep; if investigating you interrogate them, they conceal nothing; if you mistake them, they never grumble; if you are ignorant, they cannot laugh at you." One of the later minstrels, to whom is ascribed the preservation, and by some the composition, of the old ballad of Chevy Chase, thus humbles himself in a most unpoetical and undignified manner to those who fed him for his services :—

> "Now for the good cheer that I have had here
> I give you hearty thanks with bowing of my shanks,
> Desiring you by petition to grant me such commission—
> Because my name is Sheale—that both for meat and meal
> To you I may resort some time for my comfort.
> For I perceive here at all times is good cheer,
> Both ale, wine, and beer, as it doth now appear;
> I perceive, without fable, ye keep a good table.
> I can be content, if it be out of Lent,
> A piece of beef to take, my hunger to aslake;
> Both mutton and veal is good for Richard Sheale.
> Though I look so grave, I were a very knave
> If I would think scorn, either evening or morn,
> Being in hunger, of fresh salmon or congar.
> I can find in my heart with my friends to take a part
> Of such as God shall send; and thus I make an end.
> Now, farewell, good 'mine host; I thank you for your cost,
> Until another time, and thus do I end my rhyme."

But even such a humiliated ballad-maker, or ballad-singer, as poor old Richard Sheale, was the depositary of treasures of popular fiction, many of which have utterly perished, but of which a great portion of those which are still preserved are delightful even to the most refined reader. For, corrupted as they are by transmission from mouth to mouth through several centuries, they are full of high and generous sentiments, of deep pathos, of quiet humour; they carry us back into a state of society wholly different from our own, when knowledge was indeed scanty, and riches not very plentiful, but when the feelings and affections were not so wholly under the direction of worldly

wisdom, and men were brave and loving, and women
tender and confiding, with something more of earnestness
than belongs to the discreeter arrangements of modern
social life. The minstrels had indeed something to call
up the tear or the smile in every class of auditor. For
the earls and barons, the knights and squires, there were
romances and songs of chivalrous daring, such as moved
the noble heart of Sir Philip Sidney, even in the days
when the minstrel was a poor despised wanderer: "Is it
the Lyric that most displeaseth, who, with his tuned lyre
and well-accorded voice, giveth praise, the reward of virtue,
to virtuous acts? who giveth moral precepts and natural
problems? who sometimes raiseth up his voice to the
height of the heavens, in singing the lauds of the immortal
God? Certainly I must confess mine own barbarousness,
I never heard the old song of Percy and Douglas, that I
found not my heart moved more than with a trumpet, and
yet it is sung but by some blind crowder, with no rougher
voice than rude style." For those of meaner sort there
were the ballads of Robin Hood, "of whom the foolish
vulgar make lewd entertainment, and are delighted to
hear the jesters and minstrels sing them above all other
ballads." So wrote a Scottish historian in the middle of
the fourteenth century.

We have thus briefly recapitulated the popular modes
of acquiring something of a literary taste in the early
days of William Caxton. Books were rare, and difficult
to be obtained except by the wealthy. The drama did
not exist. The preachers, indeed, were not afraid to
address an indiscriminate audience with the conviction
that, although the majority were unlettered, they had
vigorous understandings, and did not require the great
truths of religion and of private and of social duty to be
adapted to any intellectual weakness or infirmity. The

national poetry, which was heard at the high festivals of
the city traders, and even descended to as lowly a popularity as that of the village circle upon the ale-bench under
the spreading elm on a summer's eve, had no essentials of
vulgarity or childishness, such as in later days have been
thought necessary for general comprehension. We were
ever a thoughtful people, a reasoning people, and · yet a
people of strong passions and unconquerable energy. A
popular literature was kept alive and preserved, however
imperfectly, before the press came to make those who had
learnt to read self-dependent in their intellectual gratifi-
cations ; and what has come down to us of the old minstrelsy, with all its inaccuracy and occasional feebleness,
shows us that the people of England, four or five centuries
ago, had a common fund of high thought upon which
a great literature might in time be reared. The very
existence of a poet like Chaucer is the best proof of the
vigour, and to a certain extent of the cultivation, of the
national mind, even in an age when books were rarities.

CHAPTER III.

CAXTON ABROAD—CAXTON'S MERCANTILE PURSUITS—RESTRICTIONS ON
TRADE—CAXTON'S COMMISSION—MERCHANTS' MARKS—BEGINNINGS OF
PRINTING — PLAYING CARDS—WOOD-ENGRAVING—BLOCK-BOOKS—MOV-
ABLE TYPES — GUTTENBERG — GUTTENBERG'S STATUE — FESTIVAL AT
MENTZ.

OBERT LARGE, the master of Caxton, became
Lord Mayor of London in 1439–40. He died
in 1441. That he was a man of considerable
substance appears by the record of his bequests
in Stow's Survey of London : " Robert Large,
mercer, mayor 1440, gave to his parish church of St. Olave,
in Surrey, two hundred pounds; to St. Margaret's, in
Lothbury, twenty-five pounds; to the poor, twenty pounds ;
to London-bridge, one hundred marks ; towards the vault-
ing over the watercourse of Walbrook, two hundred
marks ; to poor maids' marriages, one hundred marks; to
poor householders, one hundred pounds." * By his last
will he bequeathed to his servant, William Caxton, twenty
marks, a considerable sum in those days. From this
period it would seem that Caxton resided abroad. In the
first book he translated, the ' Recuyell of the Historyes of
Troye,' which bears upon the title to have been " ended
and finished in the holy city of Cologne, the 19th day
of September, the year of our Lord one thousand, four
hundred, sixty, and eleven," he says, " I have continued
by the space of thirty year for the most part in the

---

* We believe that the text of Stow, " St. Olave in *Surrey*," is a
mistake for " St. Olave in *Jewry*,"—for Robert Large was buried in
St. Olave in the Jewry, where a plated stone in the ground, in the
south aisle, recorded his death on the 24th of April, 1441.

countries of Brabant, Flanders, Holland, and Zealand."
The Rev. John Lewis, who wrote the Life of Master
William Caxton, about a century ago, says, "It has been
guessed that he was abroad as a travelling agent or factor
for the Company of Mercers, and employed by them in the
business of merchandise." Oldys adds, but certainly without any authority, "It is agreed on by those writers who
have best acquainted themselves with his story, he was
deputed and intrusted by the Mercers' Company to be
their agent or factor in Holland, Zealand, Flanders, &c.,
to establish and enlarge their correspondents, negociate
the consumption of our own, and importation of foreign
manufactures, and otherwise promote the advantage of
the said corporation in their respective merchandise."
This, indeed, was a goodly commission, if we can make
out that he ever received such,—an employment which
seems to speak of free and liberal intercourse between two
countries, each requiring the commodities of the other,
and conducting their interchange upon the sound principles
of encouraging mutual consumption, and thus producing
mutual profit. Doubtless, we may believe, upon a super-
ficial view of the matter, that the agent of the Mercers'
Company was conducting his operations with the full
authority of the government at home, and with the hearty
support of the rulers of the land in which he so long lived.
The real fact is, that for twenty of those years in which
Caxton describes himself as residing in the countries of
Brabant, Holland, and Zealand, there was an absolute
prohibition on both sides of all commercial intercourse
between England and the Duchy of Burgundy, to which
those countries were subject; and for nearly the whole
period, no English goods were suffered to pass to the
continent, except through the town of Calais; and "in
France," says Caxton, "I was never." If Caxton had any

mercantile employment at all from his Company, it was, in all probability, for the purpose of finding channels in trade that were closed up by the blind policy of the respective governments. He could not have conducted any mercantile operation in those countries, except in violation of the absurd commercial laws which would not allow the people to seek their own interest in their own way. It is by no means improbable, however, that by the connivance of the royal personages who wanted for themselves rich commodities which they could only obtain by that exchange which they denied their subjects, William Caxton was in truth an accredited smuggler for law-makers who attempted to limit the wants, and the means of satisfying the wants, of the people they governed, in deference to the prejudices of those who thought that trade could only exist under a system of the most stringent prohibition. .

While Edward the Fourth, and Charles the Good, Duke of Burgundy, were launching against each other ordinance and enactment to prevent their subjects becoming exchangers for the better supply of their respective wants, some politic understanding between these princes led them eventually to adopt a wiser system. It is pretty clear that William Caxton was one of the agents, and a principal one, in putting an end to a policy which the Duke of Burgundy said was "evermore to endure." In 1464 Edward the Fourth issued a commission to his trusty and well-beloved Richard Whitehill and William Caxton, to be his especial ambassadors, procurators, nuncios, and deputies to his most dear cousin the Duke of Burgundy for the purpose of confirming an existing treaty of commerce, or, if necessary, for making a new one. In 1466, this commission being dated in October 1464, a treaty was concluded with the Duke of Burgundy, by which the commerce between his dominions and England, which

E

had been interrupted for twenty years, was restored; and
a port of Flanders was subsequently appointed to be a
port of the English staple, as well as Calais. It is pleasant
to us to believe that this extension of a principle which
must eventually bind all nations in a common brother-
hood was effected by the good sense of a mercer of London;
who was afterwards to bestow upon his country the
blessings of an art which has been the great instrument
of that country's progress in real greatness and prosperity,
and before which all impediments to the continued course
of that prosperity—all prejudices amongst her own children,
or amongst other peoples, that make the great family of
mankind aliens and enemies, and keep them from the
enjoyment of the advantages which each might bestow
upon the other—will utterly perish. It is pleasant to us
to believe that William Caxton, the first English printer,
in his day opened the ports of one great trading community to another great trading community. When he,
the mercer's apprentice, stamped the merchant's mark
upon his master's bales, he knew not, he could not have
divined, that by this process of stamping, carried forward
by the ingenuity of many men into a new art, there would
arise consequences which would change the face of the
world. He could not imagine that he, whose education
had consisted in learning to buy wool and measure cloth,
should, by the natural course of his commercial life, be
thrown into a society where a great wonder was to fill
the minds of all men with astonishment—the multiplication of manuscripts by some new and secret process, as if
by magic; and which some men, and he probably amongst
the number, must have regarded with a higher feeling
than wonder,—with something like that prophetic view
of its consequences which have been described by the
novelist, who, perhaps more than any man, has employed

that art to the delight of all classes in every country.
We refer to the passage in Sir Walter Scott's 'Quentin
Durward,' where Louis the Eleventh of France and Marti-
valle Galeotti the astrologer speak of the invention of
printing, and the sage predicts " the lot of a succeeding
generation, on whom knowledge will descend like the first
and second rain, uninterrupted, unabated, unbounded, fer-
tilizing some grounds, and overflowing others; changing
the whole form of social life."

Merchants' Marks.

In a list of foreign goods forbidden to be imported into
this country by statute of 1464, the reader might be
surprised to find that playing-cards were of sufficient
importance, from their general use, to require that the
native manufactories should be protected in the production
of them.   Playing-cards were known in France for more
than a hundred years before this statute of Edward IV.;
so that the common notion that they were invented to
furnish amusement to an insane king, Charles VI. of
France, about 1393, is a popular error.   It is clear that
both in France and Spain at that period cards were the
amusement not only of the royal and noble inmates of
palaces, but of the burghers and the working people.   The
King of Castile, in 1387, prohibited cards altogether; and
they appear, with other games of skill and chance, to have
interfered so much with the regular labour of the artificers
of Paris, that the provost of that city, in 1397, forbade all
working people to play at tennis, bowls, nine-pins, dice,

or cards on working-days. The earliest cards were probably painted by means of a stencil, by which name we call a piece of pasteboard or plate of thin metal pierced with apertures, by which a figure is formed upon paper or other substance beneath it when fluid colour is smeared over its surface with a brush. But it has also been conjectured, from their being in the hands of the working-people, that their cheapness must have been produced by some rude application of a wood-engraving to form the outline which the stencilling process filled up with colour. There can be no doubt that cards were *printed* before the

Block and Stencil Instruments.

middle of the fifteenth century; for there is a petition extant from the Venetian *painters* to their magistracy, dated 1441, setting forth that the art and mystery of card-making and of *printing* figures, which were practised in Venice, had fallen into total decay, through the great quantity of foreign playing-cards and coloured printed figures which were brought into the city. The Germans were the great card-makers of this period; and the name by which a wood-engraver is still called in Germany, *Formschneider*, meaning figure-cutter, occurs in the town books of Nuremberg as early as 1441. Some of the early cards were very rude. Here is the Knave of Bells—for

spades, diamonds, hearts, and clubs were not then the
universal symbols.   Others called forth the skill of very
clever artists, such as he who is known as "the Master
of 1466," whose knave is a much more human knave than
the traditionary worthy whom we look upon to this hour.
When Caxton, therefore, was abroad for thirty years, he

Knave of Bells.

would unquestionably have seen every variety of these
painted bits of paper ; some rich with crimson and purple,
oftentimes painted on a golden ground, and calling forth,
like the missals, the highest art of the limner ; others
impressed with a rude outline, and daubed by the stenciller.
It appears that the impressions of the engraved cards, as
well as of most of the earlier block-prints, were taken

off by friction. This is the mode by which, even at the present day, wood-engravers take off the specimen impressions of their works called proofs. The Chinese produce their block-books in a similar manner, without the aid of a press.

But there was another application of engraved blocks, about the same period, which was approaching still nearer to the art of printing. The representations of saints and

Knave, of Master of 1466.

of scriptural histories, which the limners in the monasteries had for several centuries been painting in their missals and bibles, were copied in outline; and being divested of their brilliant colours and rich gilding, presented figures exceedingly rude in their want of proportion, and grotesque in their constrained and violent attitudes. But they were nevertheless highly popular; and as the pictures were accompanied with a few sentences from Scripture, they

probably supplied the first inducement to the laity to learn
to read, and thus prepared the way for that diffusion of
knowledge which was to accompany the invention of
printing from movable types. In the collection of Earl
Spencer there is a very curious print from a wood-block,
representing St. Christopher carrying the Infant Saviour.
This print bears the date 1423. It is probably not the
earliest specimen of the art; but it is the earliest undoubted
document which determines with precision the period when
wood-engraving was generally applied to objects of devotion. In a very few years from the date of this print the
art was carried onward to a more important object,—that
of producing a *book.*

Several of such books are now in existence, and are
known as block-books. One of them is commonly called
'Biblia Pauperum,' the Bible of the Poor. But an ingenious writer on the progress of woodcutting, in the
valuable book on that subject published by Mr. John
Jackson, has shown very clearly that this was not the
original title of the book; and he adds that it was rather
a book for the use of preachers than the laity :—" A series
of skeleton sermons ornamented with woodcuts to warm
the preacher's imagination, and stored with texts to assist
his memory." This very rare book consists of forty leaves
of small folio, each of which contains a cut in wood, with
extracts from the Scriptures, and other illustrative sentences. Of other block-books the most remarkable is
called 'Speculum Salutis,' the Mirror of Salvation. In
this performance the explanations of the text are much
fuller than in the ' Biblia Pauperum.' In addition to these
works, wooden blocks were also used to print small
manuals of grammar, called Donatuses, which were used
in schools. We present a facsimile of a woodcut from one
of the early block-books.

The Wise Men's Offering.

The use of carved blocks for the multiplication of copies
of playing-cards and devotional pictures gave birth to a
principle which has effected, and is still effecting, the most

important changes in the world. These devotional pictures had short legends or texts attached to them ; and when a text had to be printed, it was engraved in a solid piece, as well as the picture. The first person who seized upon the idea that the text or legend might be composed of separate letters capable of re-arrangement after the impressions were taken off, so as to be applied, without new cutting, to other texts and legends, had secured the principle upon which the printing art was to depend. It was easy to extend the principle from a few lines to a whole page, and from one page to many, so as to form a book; but then were seen the great labour and expense of cutting so many separate letters upon small pieces of wood or metal, and another step was required to be made before the principle was thoroughly worked out. This step consisted in the ready multiplication of the separate letters by casting metal in moulds. Lastly, instead of using the old Chinese mode of friction to produce impressions, a *press* was to be perfected. All these gradations were undoubtedly the result of long and patient experiments carried on by several individuals, who each saw the importance of the notion they were labouring to work out. It is this circumstance which has given rise to interminable controversies as to the inventors of printing, some claiming the honour for Coster of Haarlem, and some for Guttenberg of Mentz ; and, as is usual in all such disputes, it was represented that the man to whom public opinion had assigned the credit of the invention had stolen it from another, who, as is also usual in these cases, thought of it in a dream, or received it by some other mysterious revelation. The general consent of Europe now assigns the chief honour to Guttenberg.*

During the summer of 1837 a statue of John Guttenberg, by Thorwaldsen, was erected at Mentz (or Mayence), and

* See Appendix A.

on the 14th of August and the following days a festival
was held there, upon the occasion of the inauguration of the
monument. Abundant evidence has been brought forward
of late years to show that Guttenberg deserves all the
honours of having conceived, and in great part perfected,
an art which has produced the most signal effects upon the
destinies of mankind. At that festival of Mentz, at which
many hundred persons were assembled, from all parts of
Europe, to do honour to the inventor of printing, no rival
pretensions were put forward ; although many of the com-
patriots of Coster of Haarlem were present. The fine
statue of Guttenberg was opened amidst an universal
burst of enthusiasm. Never were the shouts of a vast
multitude raised on a more elevating occasion ; never
were the triumphs of intellect celebrated with greater
fervour.

Passing his life amidst the ceaseless activity that belongs
to the commerce of literature in London, the writer of this
volume felt no common interest in the enthusiasm which
the festival in honour of Guttenberg called forth throughout Germany ; and he determined to attend that celebration. The fine statue which was to be opened to public
view on the 14th of August had been erected by a general
subscription, to which all Europe was invited to contribute.
We apprehend that the English, amidst the incessant
claims upon their attention for the support of all sorts of
undertakings, whether of a national or individual character, had known little of the purpose which the good
citizens of Mentz had been advocating with unabated zeal
for several years ; and perhaps the object itself was not
calculated to call forth any very great liberality on the
part of those who are often directed in their bounties as
much by fashion as by their own convictions. Thus it
is that we have monuments out of number to warriors.

Caxton has no monument; neither has Shakspere. Be
that as it may, England literally gave nothing towards the
statue of a man whose invention has done as much as any
other single cause to make England what she is. The
remoteness of the cause may also have lessened its importance; and some people, who, without any deserts of their
own, are enjoying a more than full share of the blessings
which have been shed upon us by the progress of intellect
(which determines the progress of national wealth), have a
sort of instinctive notion that the spread of knowledge is
the spread of something inimical to the pretensions of mere
riches. We met with a lady on board the steamboat
ascending the Rhine, two days before the festival of
Mentz, who, whilst she gave us an elaborate account of
the fashionable dulness of the baths of Baden and Nassau,
and all the other German watering-places, told us by all
means to avoid Mentz during the following week, as a
crowd of low people from all parts would be there, to make
a great fuss about a printer who had been dead two
or three hundred years. The low people did assemble
in great crowds : it was computed that at least fifteen
thousand strangers had arrived to do honour to the first
printer.

The modes in which a large population displays its
enthusiasm are pretty much the same throughout the
world. If the sentiment which collects men together be
very heart-stirring, all the outward manifestations of the
sentiment harmonize with its real truth. Thus, processions, and orations, and public dinners, and pageantries,
which in themselves are vain and empty, are important
when the persons whom they collect together have one
common feeling which for the time is all-pervading. We
never saw such a popular fervour as prevailed at Mentz
at the festival of August 1837. The statue was to be

opened on Monday the 14th; but on the Sunday evening
the name of Guttenberg was rife through all the streets.
In the morning all Mentz was in motion by six o'clock;
and at eight a procession was formed to the Cathedral,
which, if it was not much more imposing than some of the
processions of trades in London and other cities, was
conducted with a quiet precision which evidenced that the
people felt they were engaged in a solemn act. The fine
old Cathedral was crowded; the Bishop of Mentz performed high Mass; the first Bible printed by Guttenberg
was displayed. What a field for reflection - was here
opened! The first Bible, in connection with the imposing
pageantries of Roman Catholicism—the Bible, in great
part a sealed book to the body of the people; the service
of God in a tongue unknown to the larger number of wor-
shippers; but that first Bible the germ of millions of
Bibles that have spread the light of Christianity throughout all the habitable globe! The Mass ended, the procession again advanced to the adjacent square, where the
statue was to be opened. Here was erected a vast amphi-
theatre, where, seated under their respective banners, were
deputations from all the great cities of Europe. Amidst
salvos of artillery the veil was removed from the statue,
and a hymn was sung by a thousand voices. Then came
orations;—then dinners — balls — oratorios—boat-races—
processions by torchlight. For three days the population
of Mentz was kept in a state of high excitement; and the
echo of the excitement. went through Germany,—and
Guttenberg! Guttenberg! was toasted in many a bumper
of Rhenish wine amidst this cordial and enthusiastic
people.

And, indeed, even in one who could not boast of belonging to the land in which printing was invented, the
universality of the mighty effects of this art, when rightly

considered, would produce almost a corresponding enthusiasm. It is difficult to look upon the great changes that have been effected during the last four centuries, and which are still in progress everywhere around us, and not connect them with printing and with its inventor. The castles on the Rhine, under whose ruins we travelled back from Mentz, perished before the powerful combinations of the people of the towns. The petty feudal despots fell, when the burghers had acquired wealth and knowledge. But the progress of despotism upon a larger scale could not have been arrested had the art of Guttenberg not been discovered. The strongholds of military power still frown over the same majestic river. The Rhine has seen its pretty fortresses crumble into decay;—Ehrenbreitstein is more strong than ever. But even Ehrenbreitstein will fall before the power of mind. The Rhine is crowded with steamboats, where the feudal lord once levied tribute upon the frail bark of the fisherman; and the approaches to the Rhine from all Germany, and from France and Belgium, have become a great series of railroads. Such communications will make war a game much more difficult to play; and when mankind are thoroughly civilized, it will never be played again. Seeing, then, what intellect has done and is doing, we may well venerate the memory of Guttenberg of Mentz.

CHAPTER IV.

THE COURT OF BURGUNDY—CAXTON A TRANSLATOR—LITERATURE OF CHIVALRY—FEUDAL TIMES—CAXTON AT THE DUCAL COURT—DID CAXTON PRINT AT BRUGES—EDWARD THE FUGITIVE—THE NEW ART.

HE "most dear" Duke of Burgundy, with whom Caxton was appointed to negotiate in 1464, was Philip, surnamed the Good. He was a wise and peaceful prince, and honourably earned his title. We know not whether Caxton was in immediate attendance upon the court of Philip from the commencement of his mission until the death of the duke in 1467; but the evidence is subsequently clear that he was about the court in some office of trust after the succession to the dukedom of the eldest son of Philip the Count of Charolois. The character of this prince was entirely opposed to that of his father; and he acquired the name of Charles le Téméraire, or the Rash. This fiery prince, whose influence in that warlike age was perhaps greater than the benignant power of his father, was not likely to have looked very favourably upon an envoy from Edward of England: for he was allied by blood on his mother's side to the house of Lancaster, and was consequently opposed to the fortunes of the house of York. The court of Burgundy was the resort of many of the adherents of that unhappy house, who had fled from England after many a vain struggle with the triumphant Edward. These fugitives are described by Comines "as young gentlemen whose fathers had been slain in England,

whom the Duke of Burgundy had generously entertained
as his relations of the house of Lancaster." Comines adds,
" Some of them were reduced to such extremity of want
and poverty before the Duke of Burgundy received them,
that no common beggar could have been in greater; I
saw one of them, who was Duke of Exeter (but he concealed his name), following the Duke of Burgundy's train
bare-foot and bare-legged, begging his bread from door to
door: this person was the next of the house of Lancaster ;
had married King Edward's sister: and being afterwards
known, had a small pension allowed him for his subsist-
ence. There were also some of the family of the Somersets,
and several others, all of them slain since, in the wars."
But the policy of Charles of Burgundy, after his accession
to the dukedom, led him to consider the ties of ancient
friendship as of far less importance than the strengthening
of his hand by an alliance with the successful house of
York. Within a year of his succession he married Margaret, sister of Edward IV. Comines says this marriage
" was principally to strengthen his alliance against the
king of France, otherwise he would never have done it,
for the love he bore to the house of Lancaster." The
establishment of Margaret as Duchess of Burgundy gave
a direction to the fortunes of William Caxton, and was in
all likelihood the proximate cause that *he* was our first
English printer.

Margaret Plantagenet was married to Charles of Burgundy at the city of Bruges, on the 3rd of July, 1468.
We have the distinct evidence of Caxton that he was
residing at Bruges some months previous to the marriage ;
that he had little to do ; and that he employed his leisure
in literary pursuits. In his ' Recuyell of the Historyes of
Troye ' it is stated in the title-page, " which said translation and work was begun in Bruges, in the county of

Flanders, the first day of March, the year of the Incar-
nation a thousand, four hundred, sixty and eight." The
prologue begins as follows : " When I remember that'
every man is bounden by the commandment and counsel
of the wise man to eschew sloth and idleness, which is
mother and nourisher of vices, and ought to put myself
unto virtuous occupation and business, then I, having no
great charge or occupation, following the said counsel,
took a French book and read therein many strange marvellous histories, wherein I had great pleasure and delight,
as well for the novelty of the same, as for the fair language
of the French, which was in prose so well and compen-
diously set and written, methought I understood the
sentence and substance of every matter. And for so much
as this book was new and late made and drawn into
French, and never had seen it in our English tongue, I
thought in myself it should be a good business to translate
it into our English, to the end that it might be had as
well in the royaume of England as in other lands, and
also for to pass therewith the time, and thus concluded in
myself to begin this said work, and forthwith took pen
and ink, and began boldly to run forth, as blind Bayard,
in this present work."

Philip de Comines, speaking of the prosperity of the
people at the time of 'the accession of Charles, says, " The
subjects of the house of Burgundy lived at that time in
great plenty and prosperity, grew proud and wallowed
in riches. . . . The expenses and habits both of women
and men were great and extravagant; their entertain-
ments and banquets more profuse and splendid than in
any other place that I ever saw." The city of Bruges
was then the great seat of this wealth and luxury. The
Flemish nobles lived here in mansions of striking archi-
tecture, some traces of which still remain. The merchants

vied with the nobles in tasteful magnificence. The canals
of Bruges were crowded with boats laden with the richest
treasures of distant lands. It was commerce that made
the inhabitants of Bruges, of Ghent, and the other great
Flemish towns so rich and powerful ; and the same commerce was the encourager of art, which even at this early
period displayed itself amongst a people naturally disposed
for its cultivation. Charles the Rash destroyed much of
this prosperity by his aptitude for war. But in the onset
of his career he fought with all the pomp and graces of
the old chivalry, and his court was the seat of such
romantic pageantries that John Paston, an Englishman
who went over with Margaret of York, writes, " As for
the duke's court, as for lords, ladies, and gentlewomen,
knights, esquires, and gentlemen, I heard never of none
like to it save King Arthur's court." It was here, without doubt, that William Caxton, the yeoman's son of the
Weald of Kent, and afterwards the mercer's apprentice of
the city of London, acquired that love for the literature of
chivalry which he displays on many occasions in his office
of translator and printer. Here he made acquaintances
that led him to the study of the romance-writers, as for
example of a worthy canon of whom he writes, " Oft times
I have been excited of the venerable man Messire Henry
Bolomyer canon of Lausanne, for to reduce for his pleasure
some histories, as well in Latin and in romance as in other
fashion written ; that is to say, of the right puissant,
virtuous, and noble Charles the Great, King of France
and Emperor of Rome, son of the great Pepin, and of his
princes and barons, as Rowland, Oliver, and other." His
zeal for this species of literature left him not in his latest
years : for in his translation of ' The Book of the Order of
Chivalry,' which was printed by him about 1484, he rises
into absolute eloquence in his address at the conclusion of

F

the volume : "Oh, ye knights of England, where is the
custom and usage of noble chivalry that was used in those
days ? What do ye now, but go to the baynes [baths] and
play at dice? And some, not well advised, use not honest
and good rule, against all order of knighthood. Leave
this, leave it ! and read the noble volumes of St. Graal,
of Lancelot, of Galaad, of Trystram, of Perse Forest, of
Percyval, of Gawayn, and many more: there shall ye see
manhood, courtesy, and gentleness. And look in latter
days of the noble acts sith the Conquest, as in King
Richard days, Cœur de Lion, Edward I., and III. and his
noble sons, Sir Robert Knolles, Sir John Hawkwode, Sir
John Chandos, and Sir Gueltiare Manny. Read Froissart;
and also behold that victorious and noble King Harry V.,
and the captains under him, his noble brethren the earls of
Salisbury, Montagu, and many other, whose names shine
gloriously by their virtuous noblesse and acts that they
did in the honour of the order of chivalry. Alas, what do
ye but sleep and take ease, and are all disordered from
chivalry ?" Caxton was dazzled, as many others were,
with the bravery and the generosity of the chivalric
character. He did not see the cruelty and pride, the
·oppression and injustice, that lurked beneath the glitter-
ing armour and the velvet mantle. Yet he was amongst
those who first helped to destroy the gross inequality upon
which chivalry was founded, by raising up the middle
classes to the possession of knowledge. There were
scenes transacting at Bruges, even at the very hour when
Margaret of York came to give her hand to Charles of
Burgundy, that must have shown him what fearful
passions were too often the companions of the courage
and graces of knighthood.

At the midsummer of 1468 Bruges presented a scene of
magnificence that was probably unequalled in those days

of costly display. On the occasion of the approaching marriage, the nobility of Charles's extensive dominions arrived from every quarter. Ambassadors were there from all Christian powers. It looked like an occasion on which men should forget that there was such a thing as war in the world; and when despotism should put on its blandest smile and its most courteous reverence for all orders of men. The Duke of Burgundy anxiously desired the presence of the Count de St. Pôl, the great Constable of France. The constable arrived, surrounded with every pomp that his pride could devise,—with trumpets and banners, with pages on foot and crowds of horsemen, and a naked sword borne before him as the symbol of sovereignty. Charles was irritated beyond measure, and refused to receive the great lord, who from that hour became his deadliest enemy. But there was something more tragic to be enacted in the midst of a population looking only for high triumphs and royal pleasures. One of the chamberlains of the Duke of Burgundy was an illegitimate son of . the Lord of Condé; he was very young, of exceeding beauty, and the most agreeable manners. He had fought by the side of the duke at the battle of Montlhéry, and was one of his most especial favourites. The youth, with that ferocious self-abandonment which was not incompatible with the gentlest manners in courts and the noblest honours in camps, committed a murder under circumstances of extraordinary aggravation. He was playing at tennis, and, the fairness of a stroke being doubtful, a bystander was called upon to decide. Deciding against the Bastard of Condé, the young man swore that he would be revenged. The bystander, who was a canon of the church, fled to his home, and the furious youth pursued him. The canon escaped, but his brother encountered the madman. Some victim must be offered up to appease his selfish rage, and

F 2

the'brother was in his path. The wretched man fell on
his knees, and, clasping his hands, begged for mercy.
Those uplifted hands were cut off in an instant, and the
sword that had been honourably drawn at Montlhéry
pierced the breast of an unoffending citizen. Such a
murder could not pass unnoticed; and yet the young man's
friends did not doubt that he would go unpunished, for he
had committed the crime in his father's lordship. Such
crimes were often committed with impunity by the great
and the powerful; and even the commonalty were un-
prepared to expect any heavier punishment than a pecuniary recompense to the relations of the murdered man.
The duke, however, had taken his determination. The
Bastard of Condé was held in arrest at the house of the
gatekeeper of the city of Bruges. Charles was solicited
on every side for pardon, and even the relations of the
deceased, having been moved by suitable presents, suppli-
cated his release; but the duke kept the matter in suspense
till Bruges was filled with his subjects from every part of
his dominions, and especially with the most powerful of
his nobles. At the instant that he was ready to depart to
meet the Lady Margaret at the neighbouring port of
Ecluse, he commanded that the young man should be
taken to the common prison, and the next morning led to
execution. Even the magistrate of the city to whom this
command was intrusted thought it impossible that the
duke should execute one so highly connected, as if he were
a common offender. The execution was delayed several
hours by the magistrate in the hope that the duke would
relent; but no respite came. The youth was carried
through the city to the place of execution, amidst the
tears of the people, who forgot his crime in his beauty.
He was beheaded, and his body divided into four quarters.
The Lord of Condé and his adherents left the city vowing

vengeance. The nobles assembled felt themselves outraged by this exercise of absolute power. Even the citizens attributed the stern decree of the duke to his indomitable pride rather than to his love of justice. Such was the prelude to the bridal festivities of the court of Burgundy; of which one who wrote an especial description in Latin says, "The sun never shone upon a more splendid ceremony since the creation of the world."

There can be no doubt that Caxton was in the direct employ of Margaret, Duchess of Burgundy. What he has told us himself of his position in her court is far more interesting than all the conjectures which his biographers have exercised upon the matter. He was in an honourable position, he was treated with confidence, he was grateful. We have already given an extract from the prologue to his 'Recuyell of·the Historyes of Troye,' which shows when and under what circumstances he commenced the translation of that work. Remembering his simpleness and unperfectness in the French and English languages (which passage we have already noticed), he continues: " When all these things came before me, after that I had made and written five or six quires, I fell in despair of this work, and purposed no more to have continued therein, and the quires laid apart; and in two years after laboured no more at this work, and was fully in will to have left it. Till on a time it fortuned that the right high, excellent, and right virtuous princess, my right redoubted lady, my Lady Margaret"—and then he gives her a host of titles—"sent for me to speak with her good grace of divers matters, among the which I let her highness have knowledge of the aforesaid beginning of this work; which anon commanded me to show the said five or six quires to her said grace. And when she had seen them, anon she found defaute [fault] in mine English, which she

commanded mo to amend, and moreover commanded mo
straightly [immediately] to continue and make an end of
tho residue then not translated. Whoso dreadful commandment I durst in no wiso disobey, becauso I am a
servant unto her said graco, and receive of her yearly fee,
and other many good and great benefits, and also hopo
many moro to receivo of her highness ; but forthwith
went and laboured in tho said translation after my simple
and poor cunning, all so nigh as I can following mino
author, meekly beseeching the bounteous highness of my
said lady, that of her benevolenco list to accept and tako
in greo [take.kindly] this simple and rude work." The
picturo which Caxton thus presents to us of his showing
his translation with an author's diffidenco to tho "dreadful" duchess, her criticism of his English, and her very
flattering command that in spito of all its faults he should
mako an end of his work, is as interesting as Froissart's
account of his literary recreations with Gaston do Foix :—
" Tho acquaintance of him and of mo was becauso I had
brought with mo a book, which I mado at tho contemplation of Winceslaus of Bohemia, Duko of Luxembourg and
of Brabant, which work was called ' Meliador,' containing
all tho songs, ballads, rondeaux, and virolays which tho
gentlo duko had mado in this timo, which, by imagination
I had gathered together : which book tho Count of Foix
was glad to see. And every night after supper I read
therein to him ; and while I read thero was nono durst
speak any word, becauso ho would I should bo well understood, wherein ho took great solaco." In both cases tho
men of letters wero received on a free and familiar footing
in tho courtly circles. In tho caso of Caxton this was
even moro honourablo to tho Lady Margaret, than tho
wolcomo which Gaston do Foix gavo to tho accomplished
knight Sir John Froissart. Caxton had no knightly

honours to recommend him; he was a plain merchant:
but he was unquestionably a man of modesty and intelli-
gence; he had travelled much; he was familiar with the
most popular literature of his day; and he desired to
extend the knowledge of it by translations into his native
language. It is difficult to say what was his exact
employment in the court of the Lady Margaret. He was
somewhat too old to partake of its light amusements, to
mingle in its gallantries, or even to prompt my lady's fool
with some word of wisdom. We have seen that four
months before Margaret of York came to Bruges he had
" no great charge or occupation," and he undertook the
translation of a considerable work " for to pass therewith
the time." It has, however, been maintained of late
years that Caxton was at this very time a printer. The
question is a curious one, and we may bestow a little
space upon its examination.

Mr. Hallam, in his ' Literature of Europe,' noticing the
progress of printing, says that several books were printed
in Paris in 1470 and 1471, adding, " But there seem to be
unquestionable proofs that a still earlier specimen of
typography is due to an English printer, the famous
Caxton. His ' Recueil des Histoires de Troye ' appears to
have been printed during the life of Philip, Duke of Burgundy, and consequently before June 15, 1467. The
place of publication, certainly within the duke's dominions, has not been conjectured. It is, therefore, by
several years the earliest printed book in the French
language. A Latin speech by Russell, ambassador of
Edward IV. to Charles of Burgundy, in 1469, is the next
publication of Caxton. This was also printed in the Low
Countries." The authority upon which the learned and
accomplished historian of the Middle Ages relies for this
statement is that of Mr. Dibdin, in his ' Typographical

Antiquities.' The French edition of the 'Recueil des Histoires de Troye' bears no printer's name, date, or place. It purports to have been composed by Raoul le Fevre, chaplain to Duke Philip de Bourgoyne, in the year 1464. The evidence that this book was printed by Caxton was summed up by Mr. Bryant, and communicated by him to Mr. Herbert, the first editor of Ames's 'Typographical Antiquities.' The Rev. Mr. Dibdin, the second editor, says that these memoranda of Mr. Bryant's "clearly prove it to have been the production of Caxton." The argument rests upon these points : that the French and English editions of Le Fevre's work have an exact conformity and likeness throughout, for not only the page itself, but the number of lines in a page, the length, breadth, and intervals of the lines, are alike in both, and the letters, great and small, are of the same magnitude. It corresponds too with 'The Game of the Chess,' printed by Caxton in England in 1474. "These considerations," says Mr. Bryant, "settle who the printer was." We venture to doubt this. Mr. Bryant has himself shown how this resemblance might be produced between books printed by Caxton, and books supposed to be printed by him, without Caxton being the actual printer. "Mentz was taken by the Duke of Saxony in the year 1462, and most of the artificers employed by John Fust, the great inventor, were dispersed abroad. I make no doubt but Caxton, who was at no great distance from Mentz, took this opportunity of making himself a master of the mystery, which he had been at much trouble and expense to obtain. This I imagine he effected by taking into pay some of Fust's servants, and settling them for a time at Cologne. Of this number probably were Pinson and Rood, Mechlin, Lettou, and Wynkyn de Worde. With the help of some of these, he printed the book [which

Wynkyn de Worde says Caxton printed] 'Bartholomeus de Prop. Rerum,' and the translation of the 'Recueil;' and probably many other books, which, being either in French or Latin, were not vendible in our country, and consequently no copies are extant here. Of all the books he printed in England, I do not remember above one in a foreign language." The calamity which drove the printers of Mentz from their homes, the storming of the city by Adolphus of Nassau, would naturally disperse their types, as well as break up their workshops. The resemblance between the doubtful books, and books undoubtedly printed by Caxton, was the resemblance of types cast in the same matrices; the spaces between the lines, as well as the form and magnitude of the letters, were produced by the letters being cast in the same mould. The resemblance would have been equally produced whether the types were used by one and the same printer, or by two printers. The typographical antiquarians say that the same types are used in the French and English works of Le Fevre and in Caxton's 'Game of Chess;' and Mr. Herbert adds, that the types are the same as those used by Fust and Schoeffer, the partners of Guttenberg. If the resemblance of types were sufficient to determine the printer of two or more books, then Fust and Schoeffer ought to be called the printers of the French 'Recueil,' as well as of the English translation which Caxton says he printed at Cologne. There can be little doubt that, when Caxton went to Cologne to be a printer in 1471, he became possessed of the types and matrices with which he printed his translation of Le Fevre, and subsequently brought to England to print his 'Game of Chess.' Another printer might have preceded him in their possession, and might have received them direct from Fust and Schoeffer. When the art ceased to be a

mystery, a profit might arise from selling the types or
multiplying the matrices. Upon these considerations we
wholly demur to the assertion, resting solely upon this
resemblance, that Caxton was a printer during the life
of Philip le Bon. The belief is entirely opposed to his
own statement, that shortly after the death of this prince
he was completely at leisure, and set about a translation
to while away his time. To be a printer in those days
was a mighty undertaking. We shall subsequently see
that he declares that he had practised and learnt the art
at great charge and expense. It is wholly unlikely, also,
that so gossiping a man, who makes a familiar friend of
his readers, telling them of almost every circumstance
that led to the printing of every book, that he in his
translation should not have said one word of being the
printer of the original work. The other book, the Latin
speech by Russell, in 1469, which has been called the
second publication of Caxton, is attributed to him absolutely upon no other grounds than the same resemblance
of type. Assuredly we cannot receive the fact of resemblance as conclusive of Caxton being the printer either in
this case or in that of the preceding. He tells us that in
1470 he was a servant receiving yearly fee from the
Duchess of Burgundy, and completed an extensive work
at her command, which he simply began " to eschew sloth
and idleness," and to put himself "unto virtuous occupation and business." When he did fairly become a
printer, he left sufficiently clear indications of his habitual
industry. We have no question how he filled up his
time when the press at Westminster was at work.

It was in the autumn of 1470, when Master William
Caxton would appear to have been busily labouring in
some silent turret of the palace at Bruges, upon his translation of Raoul le Fevre, that an event occurred, of all

others the most calculated to spread consternation in the court of Burgundy, and to make the bold duke feel that in abandoning his family alliance with the house of Lancaster he had not done the politic thing which he anticipated. Edward IV., who had sat for some years with tolerable quiet upon the English throne, to which he had fought his way in many a battle-field with prodigious bravery, suddenly arrived at Bruges, in the October of 1470, a discrowned fugitive. He made his escape from the overwhelming inroad of the power of Warwick, "attended," says Comines, "by seven or eight hundred men without any clothes but what they were to have fought in, no money in their pockets, and not one in twenty of them knew whither they were going." He, the most beautiful man of the time, as Comines describes him,—who for twelve or thirteen years of prosperity had lived a life of the most luxurious gratification,—he arrived at Bruges, after being chased by privateers, and with difficulty rescued from their hands, so poor that he "was forced to give the master of the ship for his passage a gown lined with martens." At Bruges, then, did this fugitive remain nearly five months, when he again leaped into his throne, in the following April, with a triumphant boldness which has only one parallel in modern history,—that of the march of Napoleon from Elba. In May, 1471, he addressed a letter in French to the nobles and burgomasters of Bruges, thanking them for the courtesy and hospitality he had received from them during his exile. Edward was of a sanguine temper; and, however depressed in fortune, was not likely, during those five months of humiliation, to have doubted that in good time he should regain the throne. He was of an easy and communicative disposition; and would naturally confer with his sister and her confidential servants upon his plans and prospects. Comines says, "King Edward told me

that, in all the battles which he had gained, his way was,
when the victory was on his side, to mount on horseback,
and cry out to save the common soldiers, and put the
gentry to the sword." We mention this to show that he
was not indisposed to talk of himself and his doings with
those whom he met during his exile. It is more than
probable, then, that he had the same sort of free communication with his countryman Caxton. It was at this period
that the progress of the art of printing must have been a
subject of universal interest. The merchants of Bruges
had commercial intercourse with all the countries of
Europe ; and they would naturally bring to the court of
Burgundy some specimens of that art which was already
beginning to create a new description of commerce. From
Mentz, Bamberg, Cologne, Strasburg, and Augsburg they
would bring some of the Latin and German Bibles which,
from 1461 to 1470, had issued from the presses of those
cities. The presses of Italy, and especially of Rome, of
Venice, and of Milan, had, during the same period, sent
forth books, and more particularly classical works, in great
abundance. The art had made such rapid progress in
Italy, that in the first edition of St. Jerome's Epistles,
printed in 1468, the Bishop of Aleria thus addresses Pope
Paul II. : " It was reserved for the times of your holiness
for the Christian world to be blessed with the immense
advantages resulting from the art of printing; by means
of which, and with a little money, the poorest person
may collect together a few books. It is a small testimony
of the glory of your holiness, that the volumes which
formerly scarcely an hundred golden crowns would purchase may now be procured for twenty and less, and these
well-written and authentic ones." It is pretty clear that
Caxton, when he began his translation of the ' Histories of
Troy,' had some larger circulation in view than could be

obtained by the medium of transcription : " I thought in
myself it should be a good business to translate it into our
English, to the end that it might be had as well in the
royaume of England as in other lands." It is also probable
that he was moving about in search of the best mode
of printing it ; for he says, at the end of the second book
of the ' Recueil,' " And for as much as I suppose the said
two books be not had before this time in our English
language, therefore I had the better will to accomplish the
said work ; which work was begun in Bruges, and continued in Gaunt [Ghent], and finished in Cologne, in time
of the troublous world, and of the great divisions being
and reigning as well in the royaumes of England and
France as in all other places universally through the
world, that is to wit, the year of our Lord one thousand,
four hundred, and seventy-one." But he further says,
with reference to his translation of the third book, which
he doubted about doing, " because that I have now good
leisure, being in Cologne, and have none other thing to do
at this time in eschewing of idleness, mother of all vices,
I have deliberated in myself of the contemplation of my
said redoubted lady, to take this labour in hand."[We
shall presently see when Caxton became, or at any rate
avowed himself to have become, a printer. Up to this
point we see him only as a translator, a man of leisure, and
not one learning a new and difficult craft.] But we see him
moving about from Bruges to Ghent, from Ghent to
Cologne, without any distinct or specified object. There
can be little doubt, we believe, that he was endeavouring
to make himself acquainted with the new art, still in great
measure a secret art, the masters of which required to be
approached with considerable caution. That the presence
of Edward IV. in Flanders, during a period when Caxton
might readily have had access to his person, might have

led him to believe that the time would come when, under
the patronage of the restored prince, he might carry the
art to London, is not an improbable conjecture. Amongst
the companions of Edward's exile was his brother-in-law,
the celebrated Lord Rivers. This brave and accomplished
young nobleman subsequently translated a book called
'The Dictes and Sayings of Philosophers,' which Caxton
printed at Westminster, in 1477. The printer has added
an appendix to this translation, from which we collect that
the noble author and his literary printer were upon terms
of mutual confidence and regard : " At such time as he had
accomplished this said work, it liked him to send it to me
in certain quires to oversee. . . . . And so afterward I
came unto my said lord, and told him how I had read and
seen his book, and that he had done a meritorious deed in
the labour of the translation thereof. . . . . Then my
said lord desired me to oversee it, and, where as I should
find fault, to correct it, wherein I answered unto his lordship that I could not amend it. . . . . Notwithstanding
he willed me to oversee it." Earl Rivers, then Lord Scales,
was also at Bruges upon the occasion of the Lady Margaret's marriage. Employed, therefore, by the the Duchess
of Burgundy, the sister of Edward IV., and honoured with
the confidence of Earl Rivers, his brother-in-law, we may
reasonably believe that the presence of Edward at Bruges
in 1470–71 might have had some influence upon the determination of Caxton to learn and practise the new art of
printing, and to carry it into England, if the " troublous
times " could afford him occasion. We have distinct evidence that Edward IV. gave a marked encouragement to
the labours of Caxton as a translator, in a book printed by
him without any date, 'The Life of Jason,' written, as were
the ' Histories of Troy,' by Raoul le Fevre, in which Caxton
says in his prologue, " For as much as late by the com-

mandment of the right high and noble princess my Lady
Margaret, &c., I translated a book out of French in English,
named 'Recueil,' &c. . . . . Therefore, under the protection and sufferance of the most high, puissant, and Christian
king, my most dread natural liege, Lord Edward, &c., I
intend to translate the said book of the 'Histories of
Jason.'" The expression "for as much as late by the
commandment," &c., brings the date of the 'Histories of
Jason' close to that of the 'Histories of Troy,' and points
out the probability that the protection and sufferance of
Edward was afforded to Caxton when the king was a
fugitive at the court of Burgundy. In the 'Issues of the
Exchequer' there is the following entry of a payment on
the 15th of June, in the 19th of Edward IV.: "To William
Caxton, in money paid to his own hands, in discharge of
twenty pounds which the lord the king commanded to be
paid to the same William for certain causes and matters
performed by him for the said lord the king." This is
eight years after the period of Edward's exile, being in
1479. But as the productions of Caxton's press were very
prolific at this time, we may believe that the payment of
such a large sum for certain causes and matters performed
for the king was in some degree connected with his labours
in the introduction of printing into England,—a payment
not improbably postponed for obligations incurred, and
promises granted, at an earlier period.

CHAPTER V.

RAPIDITY OF PRINTING—WHO THE FIRST ENGLISH PRINTER—CAXTON THE FIRST ENGLISH PRINTER—FIRST ENGLISH PRINTED BOOK—DIFFICULTIES OF THE FIRST PRINTERS—ANCIENT BOOKBINDING—THE PRINTER A PUBLISHER—CONDITIONS OF CHEAPNESS IN BOOKS.

T the end of the third book of Caxton's translation of the 'Recuyell of the Historyes of Troye,' which we have so often quoted, is the following most curious passage: "Thus end I this book, which I have translated after mine author, as nigh as God hath given me cunning, to whom be given the laud and praises. And for as much as in the writing of the same my pen is worn, mine hand weary and not stedfast, mine eyen dimmed with overmuch looking on the white paper, and my courage not so prone and ready to labour as it hath been, and that age creepeth on me daily and feebleth all the body; and also because I have promised to divers gentlemen and to my friends to address to them as hastily as I might this said book, therefore I have practised and learned, at my great charge and dispense [expense], to ordain this said book in print, after the manner and form as you may here see; and is not written with pen and ink as other books are, to the end that every man may have them at once. For all the books of this story named the 'Recuyell of the Historyes of Troye,' thus imprinted as ye here see, were begun in one day, and also finished in one day. Which book I presented to my said redoubted lady as afore is said, and

she hath well accepted it and largely rewarded me." It
was customary for the first printers, which is not according
to the belief that they wanted to palm their printed
books off as manuscripts, to state that they were not
drawn or written with a pen and ink. Udalricus Gallus,
who printed at Rome about 1470, says, "I, Udalricus
Gallus, without pen or pencil have imprinted this book."
But he further says of himself at the end of one of his
books, "I printed thus much in a day; it is not written
in a year." It has been held that Caxton uses a purely
marvellous and hyperbolical mode of expression, when he
says, "All the books of this story, thus imprinted as ye
here see, were begun in one day and finished in one day."
Dr. Dibdin inquires what Caxton meant "by saying that
the book was begun and finished in one day? Did he
wish his countrymen to believe that the translation of
Le Fevre's book was absolutely printed in twenty-four
hours?" Dr. Dibdin truly holds the thing to be im-
practicable, because the book consisted of seven hundred
and seventy-eight folio pages. Such feats have been done
with the large capital and division of labour of modern
times; but to begin and finish such a book in one day in
the fifteenth century was certainly an impossibility. We
venture to think that Caxton says nothing of the sort.
He puts with great force and justice the chief advantages
of printing,—the rapidity with which many copies could
be produced at once. He promised, he says, to divers
gentlemen and friends to address to them as hastily as
he might this book. There were many who wanted the
book. The transcribers could not supply their wants.
He could not multiply copies himself with his pen, for
his hand was weary and his eyes dim. He learned, therefore, to ordain the book in print, to the end that all his
friends might have the books at the same time,—that

G

every man might have them at once; and to explain this,
he says, all the books thus imprinted were begun in one
day. If he printed a hundred copies, each of the hundred
copies was begun at the same time; a hundred sheets,
each sheet forming a portion of each copy, were printed
off in one day,—and in the same way were they also
finished in one day. He does not say, as Dr. Dibdin in-
terprets the passage, that *the book* was begun and finished
in one day,—one and the same day,—but that *all* the
books were begun on one day, and all the books were
finished on another day. His expression is not very
clear, but his meaning is quite apparent. This was the
end that he sought to obtain at great charge and expense;
this is the end which has been more and more obtained
at every step forward in the art of printing,—the rapid
multiplication of copies, so that all men may have them
at once.

The place where Caxton learned the art of printing,
and the persons of whom he first learned it, are not
shown in any of his voluminous prologues and prefaces.
But an extraordinary statement was published in the
year 1664, by a person of the name of Richard Atkyns,
who sought to prove that printing was a royal prerogative, because, as he says, the art was first brought into
England at the cost of the crown. His narrative is held
to be altogether a fiction; for the document upon which
he rests it was never forthcoming, and no person has ever
testified to the knowledge of it, except Richard Atkyns
himself, who laboured hard to obtain a patent from the
crown for the sole printing of law-books, upon the ground
which he attempts to take of the crown having brought
printing into England. " Thomas Bourchier, Archbishop
of Canterbury, moved the then king, Henry VI., to use
all possible means for procuring a printing-mould, for so

it was then called, to be brought into this kingdom. The king, a good man, and much given to works of this nature, readily hearkened to the motion; and taking private advice how to effect this design, concluded it could not be brought about without great secrecy, and a considerable sum of money given to such person or persons as would draw off some of the workmen from Haarlem in Holland, where John Guttenberg had newly invented it, and was himself personally at work. It was resolved that less than one thousand marks would not produce the desired effect: towards which sum the said archbishop presented the king with three hundred marks. The money being now prepared, the management of the design was committed to Mr. Robert Turnour, who then was keeper of the robes to the king, and a person most in favour with him of any of his condition. Mr. Turnour took to his assistance Mr. Caxton, a citizen of good abilities, who, trading much into Holland, might be a creditable pretence, as well for his going as staying in the Low Countries. Mr. Turnour was in disguise, his beard and hair shaven quite off, but Mr. Caxton appeared known and public. They having received the sum of one thousand marks, went first to Amsterdam, then to Leyden, not daring to enter Haarlem itself; for the town was very jealous, having imprisoned and apprehended divers persons, who came from other parts for the same purpose. They stayed till they had spent the whole one thousand marks in gifts and expenses. So as the king was fain to send five hundred marks more, Mr. Turnour having written to the king that he had almost done his work, a bargain, as he said, being struck between him and two Hollanders for bringing off one of the workmen, who should sufficiently discover and teach the new art. At last, with much ado, they got off one of the under

workmen, whose name was Frederick Corsells, or rather
Corsellis; who late one night stole from his fellows in
disguise, into a vessel prepared before for that purpose;
and so the wind, favouring the design, brought him safe
to London. It was not thought so prudent to set him on
work at London, but by the archbishop's means, who
had been Vice-chancellor and afterwards Chancellor of
the University of Oxon, Corsellis was carried with a
guard to Oxon, which constantly watched to prevent
Corsellis from any possible escape, 'till he had made good
his promise, in teaching how to print. So that at Oxford
printing was first set up in England." This is certainly
an extraordinary story, and one which upon the face of it
has traces of inconsistency, if not of imposture. Richard
Atkyns says that a certain worthy person " did present
me with a copy of a record and manuscript in Lambeth
House, heretofore in his custody, belonging to the See,
and not to any particular Archbishop of Canterbury.
The substance whereof was this; though I hope, for
public satisfaction, the record itself in its due time will
appear." The record itself did never appear, and, though
diligently sought for, could never be found. But Atkyns
further stated that the same most worthy person who
gave him the copy of the record, trusted him with a book
" printed at Oxon, A.D. 1468, which was three years before
any of the recited authors [Stow and others] would allow
it [printing] to be in England." He does not mention
the book; but there is such a book, and it is entitled 'Expositio Sancti Ieronimi in Simbolum, ad Papam Lauren-
tiam;' and at the end, 'Explicit Expositio, &c., Impressa
Oxonie, et finita Anno Dom. MCCCCLXVIII, xvii die Decem-
bris.' Anthony Wood repeats the story of Atkyns in his
'History of the University of Oxford;' and he adds,
" And thus the mystery of printing appeared ten years

sooner in the University of Oxford than at any other
place in Europe, Haarlem and Mentz excepted. Not long
after there were presses set up in Westminister, St. Albans,
Worcester, and other monasteries of note. After this
manner printing was introduced into England, by the
care of Archbishop Bourchier, in the year of Christ 1464,
and the third of King Edward IV." Wood's version of
the story makes it a little, a very little, more credible, for
it brings it nearer to the time when the newly-discovered
art of printing might have attracted some attention in
England. But even in 1464 there were, with scarcely
more than one exception, no printed books known in
Europe but the first productions of the press at Mentz.
The story of Caxton going to Haarlem in the time of
Henry the Sixth, that is, in some year previous to 1461,
must altogether be a fabrication, or a mistake. The
accounts that would ascribe the invention of printing to
Laurence Coster, of Haarlem, set up a legendary story that
John Fust, or John Guttenberg (not the real Guttenberg,
but an elder brother), stole the invention from Coster and
carried it to Mentz in 1442. If Caxton, therefore, went
to Haarlem in Holland, with a companion, in disguise, to
learn the art of printing, he must have gone there before
1442; for the story holds that Coster was not only robbed
of his secret, but of his types, and gave up printing, in
despair to his more fortunate spoiler. Bourchier was not
Archbishop of Canterbury till 1454. We may be sure,
therefore, that, wherever Caxton went to learn the art of
printing at an earlier period than is generally supposed, he
did not go to Haarlem in Holland. Substitute Mentz for
Haarlem, and Atkyns's story is more consistent. It is by
no means improbable that Henry the Sixth and Cardinal
Bourchier might have seen the magnificent Latin Bible,
called the Mazarine Bible, which was printed by Gutten-

berg, Schoeffer, and Fust, and is held to have appeared
about 1455. Of this noble book Mr. Hallam says, " It is a
very striking circumstance, that the high-minded inventors
of this great art tried at the very outset so bold a flight
as the printing an entire Bible, and executed it with
astonishing success. It was Minerva leaping on earth in
her divine strength and radiant armour, ready at the
moment of her nativity to subdue and destroy her enemies."
The king and the archbishop might have desired that
England should learn the art of executing so splendid a
work as the first Bible. At that period we know that
Caxton was residing abroad, and he was a fit person to be
selected for such a commission. But kings at that day were
scarcely better supplied with money than their subjects ;
and if Henry the Sixth had sent to Mr. Robert Turnour or
Mr. William Caxton seven hundred marks at one time and
five hundred at another, the gifts must have been registered
with all due formality. We have the Exchequer registers
of Henry the Sixth and his great rival ; and although we
learn that Edward the Fourth gave Caxton twenty pounds,
neither his name nor that of Mr. Turnour, nor even of the
archbishop, is associated with any bounty of Henry the
Sixth. We may, therefore, safely conclude, with Dr.
Conyers Middleton, with regard to all this story, that
" Mr. Atkyns, a bold vain man, might be the inventor of
it, having an interest in imposing upon the world, to
confirm his argument that printing was of the prerogative
royal, in opposition to the stationers ; against whom he
was engaged in expensive lawsuits, in defence of the
king's patents, under which he claimed some exclusive
powers of printing." The date of 1468 on the Oxford
book is reasonably concluded to have been a typographical
error. There are niceties in the printing of that book
which did not belong to the earliest stages of the art; and

the same type and manner of printing are seen in Oxford books printed immediately after 1478. The probability therefore is, that an X was omitted in the Roman numerals.

We could scarcely avoid detailing this story, apocryphal as the whole matter is upon the face of it, because the claims of Oxford to the honour of the first printing-press were once the subject of a fierce controversy. The honest antiquarian Oldys complains most bitterly of Richard Atkyns, " How unwarrantably he robbed Master Caxton of the honour, wherewith he had long been, by the suffrage of all learned men, undeniably invested, of first introducing and practising this most scientifical invention among us." But had this story been true, Caxton would not have been robbed of his glory. He would still have been what Leland, writing within half a century of his death, calls him, " Angliæ Prototypographus "—the first printer of England. For it is not the man who is the accidental instrument of introducing a great invention, and then pursues it no further, who is to have the fame of its promulgation. It is he who by patient and assiduous labour acquires the mastery of a new principle, sees afar off the high objects to which it may be applied, carries out its details with persevering courage, is not deterred by failure nor satisfied with partial success, works for a great purpose through long years of anxiety, is careless of honours or rewards, and finally does accomplish all and much more than he proposed, planting the tree, training it, rejoicing in its good fruit,—he it is that is the real first introducer and practiser of a great scientific invention, even though some one may have preceded him in some similar attempt—an experiment, but not a perfect work. We may well believe that, for some ten years of his residence abroad, the knowledge that a new art was discovered, promising such

mighty results as that of printing, must have excited the
deepest interest in the mind of Caxton. He says himself,
in his continuation of the Polychronicon, " About this time
[1455] the craft of imprinting was first found in Mogunce
in Almayne." During his residence at the court of Burgundy he would see the art multiplying around him.
Italy, where it most extensively flourished before 1470,
was too distant for his personal inspection. Bamberg,
Augsburg, and Strasburg brought it nearer to him. But
Cologne, where Conrad Winters set up a press about 1470,
was very near at hand. A few days' journey would place
him within the walls of the holy city of the Rhine.
Cologne, we .have no doubt, fixed the employment of the
remainder of his life; and made the London mercer, whose
name, like the names of many other good and respectable
men, would have held no place in the memory of the
world but for the art he learnt in his latter years,—
Cologne rendered the name of Caxton a bright and venerable name;— a name that even his countrymen, who are
accustomed chiefly to raise columns and statues to the
warlike defenders of their country, will one day honour
amongst the heroes who have most successfully cultivated
the arts of peace, and by high talent and patient labour
have rendered it impossible that mankind should not
steadily advance in the acquisition of knowledge and
virtue, and in the consequent amelioration of the lot of
every member of the family of mankind, at some period,
present or remote.

The provost of the city of Mentz, on the occasion of the
festival of Guttenberg, published an address full of German
enthusiasm, at which we may be apt to smile, but which
breathes a spirit of reverence for the higher concerns of
our being which we might profitably engraft upon the
practical good sense on which we pride ourselves. He

says, "If the mortal who invented that method of fixing
the fugitive sounds of words which we call the alphabet
has operated upon mankind like a divinity, so also has
Guttenberg's genius brought together the once isolated
inquirers, teachers, and learners—all the scattered and
divided efforts for extending God's kingdom over the whole
civilized earth—as though beneath one temple.   Guttenberg's invention, not a lucky accident, but the golden
fruit of a well-considered idea—an invention made with
a perfect consciousness of its end—has above all other
causes, for more than four centuries, urged forward and
established the dominion of science: and what is of the
most importance, has immeasurably advanced the mental
formation and education of the people.   This invention, a
true intellectual sun, has mounted above the horizon, first
of the European Christians, and then of the people of other
climes and other faiths to an ever-enduring morning.   It
has made the return of barbarism, the isolation of mankind, the reign of darkness, impossible for all future times.
It has established a public opinion, a court of moral judi-
cature common to all civilized nations, whatever natural
divisions may separate them, as much as for the provinces
of one and the same state.   In a word, it has formed
fellow labourers at the never-resting loom of Christian
European civilization in every quarter of the world, in
almost every island of the ocean."

Filled with some such strong belief, although perhaps
a vague belief, of the blessings which printing might
bestow upon his own country, we may view William Caxton
proceeding, about the end of 1470, to the city of Cologne,
resolved to acquire the art of which he had seen some of
the effects, without stint of labour or expense.   That he
was an apt and diligent scholar his after works abundantly
prove.

The first book printed in the English language, the 'Recueil of the Histories of Troy,' which we have so often noticed, does not bear upon the face of it when and where it was printed. That it was printed by Caxton we can have no doubt, because he says, "I have practised and learned, at my great charge and dispense, to ordain this said book in print." He tells us, too, in the title-page, that the *translation* was finished at Cologne, in September, 1471. That Caxton printed at Cologne we have tolerably clear evidence. There is a most curious book of Natural History, originally written in Latin by Bartholomew Glanvill, a Franciscan friar of the fourteenth century, commonly known as Bartholomæus. A translation of this book, which is called 'De Proprietatibus Rerum,' was printed in England by Wynkyn de Worde, who was an assistant to Caxton in his printing-office at Westminster, and there succeeded to him. In some quaint stanzas which occur in this edition, and which appear to be written either by or in the name of the printer, are these lines, which we copy, in the first instance, exactly following the orthography and non-punctuation of the original :—

> " And also of your charyte call to remembraunce
> The soule of William Caxton first pryter of this boke
> Jn laten tonge at Coleyn hyself to auaūce
> That euery well disposyd man may theron loke."

That we are asked to call to remembrance the soul of William Caxton is perfectly clear; but how are we to read the subsequent members of the sentence? The most obvious meaning appears to be that William Caxton was the first printer of this book in the Latin tongue; that he printed it at Cologne; and that his object in printing it was to advance or profit himself, in addition to his desire that every well-disposed man might look upon it. But there is another interpretation of these words, which is

certainly not a forced one : that William Caxton was the
first printer of this book, the English book, and that
the object of his printing it was to advance himself in
the Latin tongue at Cologne. " This book " would appear
then to be, this English book, this same book. If a copy
of this book, whether in Latin or English, printed at
Cologne at so early a period, could be found, the question
would be set at rest. There is a Latin edition printed at
Cologne, in 1481, by John Koelhoff; and there is an
edition in Latin without date or place. The first English
edition known is that by Wynkyn de Worde, and that
translation was made much earlier than the time of Caxton,
by John de Trevisa. Caxton could scarcely have been
said to have desired to have advanced himself in the Latin
tongue, unless he had translated the book as well as printed
it. The mere fact of superintending workmen who set
up the types in Latin would have done little to advance
his knowledge of the language. We believe, therefore,
that we must receive the obscure lines of Wynkyn de
Worde as evidence that Caxton did print at Cologne, and
that he undertook the Latin edition of Bartholomæus as a
commercial speculation, " himself to advance," or profit.

   And, indeed, when we look at the state of England after
the return of Edward IV. from his exile,—the " great
divisions " of which Caxton himself speaks,—we may
consider that he acted with discretion in conducting his
first printing operations in a German city. It must be
also borne in mind that this was by far the readiest mode
to obtain a competent knowledge in the new art. Had he
come over to England with types and presses, and even
with the most skilful workmen, the probability is that
the man of letters who, two or three years before, had
little or nothing to do in his attendance upon the Bur-
gundian court, would have ill succeeded in so complicated

and difficult a commercial enterprise. Lambinet, a French bibliographical writer, tells us that Melchior de Stamham, wishing to establish a printing-office at Augsburg, engaged a skilful workman of the same town, of the name of Sauerloch. He employed a whole year in making the necessary preparations for his office. He bought five presses, of the materials of which he constructed five other presses. He cast pewter types, and, having spent a large sum, seven hundred and two florins, in establishing his office, began working in 1473. He died before he had completed one book : heartbroken, probably, at the amount of capital he had sunk; for his unfinished book was sold off at a mere trifle, and his office broken up. This statement, which rests upon some ancient testimony, shows us something of the difficulties which had to be encountered by the early printers. They had to do everything for themselves ; to construct the materials of their art, types, presses, and every other instrument and appliance. When Caxton began to print at Cologne, he probably had the means of obtaining a set of moulds from some previous printer,—what are called strikes from the punches that form the original matrices. The writers upon typography seem to assume the necessity of every one of the old printers cutting his punches anew, and shaping his letters according to his own notions of proportionate beauty. That the great masters of their art, the first inventors, the Italian printers, the Alduses, the Stephenses, pursued this course is perfectly clear. But when printing ceased to be a mystery, about 1462, it is more than probable that those who tried to set up a press, especially in Germany, either bought a few types of the more established printers, or obtained a readier means of casting types than that of cutting new punches,—a difficult and expensive operation. Thus we believe the attempts to assign a book without a printer's name to some printer whose types that book resembles can be little relied upon. Caxton's types are held to be like the type of this printer and the type of that; and it is said that he copied the types, with the objection added that he did not copy the best models. What should have prevented him buying the types from the continent, as every English printer did until the middle of the last century? or at any rate what should have prevented him buying copies of the moulds which other printers were using? The bas-relief upon Thorwaldsen's statue of Guttenberg exhibits the first printer examining a matrix. But all the difficulties in the formation of the first matrix overcome, we may readily see that, at every stage, the art of making fusile types would become easier and simpler, till at length the division of labour should be perfectly applied to type-making, and the mere casting of a letter, as each letter is cast singly, exhibit one of the most rapid and beautiful pieces of handiwork that the arts can show.

. But the type obtained, Caxton would still have much to do before his office was furnished. We have seen how Melchior of Augsburg set about getting his presses: " He bought of John Schuesseler five presses, which cost him seventy-three Rhenish florins : he constructed with these materials five other smaller presses." To those who know what a well-adjusted machine the commonest printing-press now in use is, it is not easy at first to conceive what is meant by saying that Melchior bought five presses, and made five other presses out of the materials. The solution is this : in all probability this printer of Augsburg bought five old wine-presses, and, using the screws, cut them down and adapted them to the special purpose for which he designed them. The earliest printing-press was nothing more than a common screw-press,—such as a cheese-press, or a napkin-press,—with a contrivance for running the *form* of types under the screw after the *form* was inked. It is evident that this mode of obtaining an impression must have been very laborious and very slow. As the screw must have come down upon the types with a dead pull,—that is, as the table upon which the types were placed was solid and unyielding,—great care must have been required to prevent the pressure being so hard as to injure the face of the letters.

A famous printer, Jodocus Badius Ascensianus, has exhibited his press in the title-page of a book printed by him in 1498. Up to the middle of the last century this rude press was in use in England; although the press of an ingenious Dutch mechanic, Blaew,—in which the pressure was rapidly communicated from the screw to the types, and all the parts of the press were yielding so as to produce a sharp but not a crushing impression,—was gradually superseding it. The early printers manufactured their own ink, so that Caxton had to learn the art of ink-making. The ink was applied to the types by balls, or dabbers, such as one of the men holds who is working the press of Badius. Such dabbers were universally used in printing forty years ago. As the ancient weaver was expected to make his own loom, so, even this short time since, the division of labour was so imperfectly applied to printing, that the pressman was expected to make his own balls. A very rude and nasty process this was. The sheepskins, called pelts, were prepared in the printing-office, where the wool with which they were stuffed was also carded ; and these balls, thus manufactured by a man whose general work was entirely of a different nature, required the expenditure of at least half an hour's labour every day in a very disagreeable operation, by which they were kept soft.

There were many other little niceties in the home construction of the materials for printing which Caxton would
necessarily have to learn.   But in the earlier stages of an
art requiring such nice arrangement, both in the depart-
ments of the compositor, or setter-up of the type, and of
the pressman, it is quite clear that many things which,

Ancient Press.

by the habit of four centuries, have become familiar and
easy in a printing-office, would be exceedingly difficult to
be acquired by the first printers.   Rapidity in the work
was probably out of the question.   Accidents must constantly have occurred in wedging up the single letters
tightly in pages and sheets; and when one looks at the

regularity of the inking of these old books, and the beautiful accuracy with which the line on one side of a page falls on the corresponding line on the other side (called by printers " register "), we may be sure that with very imperfect mechanical means an amount of care was taken in working off the sheets which would appear ludicrous to a modern pressman. The higher operation of a printing-office, which consists in reading the proofs, must have been in the first instance full of embarrassment and difficulty. A scholar was doubtless employed to test the accuracy of the proofs; probably some one who had been previously employed to overlook the labours of the transcribers. Fierce must have been the indignation of such a one during a course of painful experience, when he found one letter presented for another, letters and even syllables and words omitted, letters topsy-turvy, and even actual substitutions of one word for another. These are almost unavoidable consequences of the mechanical operation of arranging movable types, so entirely different from the work of the transcriber. The corrector of the press would not understand this; and his life would not be a pleasant one. Caxton was no doubt the corrector of his own press; and well for him it was that he brought to his task the patience, industry, and good temper which are manifest in his writings.

But the ancient printer had something more to do before his manufacture was complete. He was a bookbinder as well as a printer. The ancient books, manuscript as well as printed, were wonderful specimens of patient labour. The board, literally a wooden board, between which the leaves were fastened, was as thick as the panel of a door. This was covered with leather, sometimes embossed with the most ingenious devices. There were large brass nails, with ornamented heads, on the outside of this cover, with

magnificent corners to the lids. In addition, there were
clasps. The back was rendered solid with paste and glue,
so as to last for centuries. Erasmus says of such a book,
"As for Thomas Aquinas's Secunda Secundæ, no man can
carry it about, much less get it into his head." An ancient
woodcut shows us the binder hammering at the leaves to
make them flat, and a lad sewing the leaves in a frame
very like that still in use. Above are the books flying in
the air in all their solid glory.

But the most difficult labour of the ancient printer, and
that which would necessarily constitute the great distinction between one printer and another, was yet to come.
He had to sell his books when he had manufactured them,
for there was no division of the labour of publisher and
printer in those days. His success would of course much
depend upon the quality of his books; upon their adapta-
tion to the nature of the demand for books; upon their
accuracy; upon their approach to the beauty of the old
manuscripts. But he had to incur the risk common to all
copying processes, whether the thing produced be a medal
or a book, of expending a large certain sum before a single
copy could be produced. The process of printing, compared with that of writing, is a cheap process as ordinarily
conducted; but the condition of cheapness is this,—that a
sufficient number of copies of any particular book may be
reckoned upon as salable, so as to render the proportion
of the first expense upon a single copy inconsiderable. If
it were required even at the present time to print a single
copy, or even three or four copies only, of any literary
work, the cost of printing would be greater than the cost
of transcribing. It is when hundreds, and especially thousands, of the same work are demanded, that the great
value of the printing-press in making knowledge cheap is
particularly shown. It is probable that the first printers

did not take off more than two or three hundred, if so many, of their works; and, therefore, the earliest printed books must have been still dear, on account of the limited number of their readers. Caxton, as it appears by a passage in one of his books, was a cautious printer; and required something like an assurance that he should sell enough of any particular book to repay the cost of producing it. In his 'Legend of Saints' he says, "I have submysed [submitted] myself to translate into English the 'Legend of Saints,' called 'Legenda aurea' in Latin; and William, Earl of Arundel, desired me—and promised to take a reasonable quantity of them—and sent me a worshipful gentleman, promising that my said lord should during my life give and grant to me a yearly fee, that is to note, a buck in summer and a doe in winter." Caxton, with his sale of a reasonable quantity, and his summer and winter venison, was more fortunate than others of his brethren, who speculated upon a public demand for books without any guarantee from the great and wealthy. Sweynheim and Pannartz, Germans who settled in Rome, and there printed many beautiful editions of the Latin Classics, presented a petition to the Pope, in 1471, which contains the following passage: "We were the first of the Germans who introduced this art, with vast labour and cost, into your holiness' territories, in the time of your predecessor; and encouraged by our example other printers to do the same. If you peruse the catalogue of the works printed by us, you will admire how and where we could procure a sufficient quantity of paper, or even rags, for such a number of volumes. The total of these books amounts to 12,475,— a prodigious heap,—and intolerable to us, your holiness' printers, by reason of those unsold. We are no longer able to bear the great expense of housekeeping, for want of buyers; of which there cannot be a more flagrant proof

than that our house, though otherwise spacious enough, is
full of quire-books, but void of every necessary of life."
For some years after the invention of printing, many of
the ingenious, learned, and enterprising men who devoted
themselves to the new art which was to change the face of
society were ruined, because they could not sell cheaply
unless they printed a considerable number of a book; and
there were not readers enough to take off the stock which
they thus accumulated. In time, however, as the facilities
for acquiring knowledge which printing afforded created
many readers, the trade of printing books became one of less
general risk; and dealers in literature could afford more
and more to dispense with individual patronage, and rely
upon the public demand.

CHAPTER VI.

THE PRESS AT WESTMINSTER — THEOLOGICAL BOOKS — CHARACTER OF
CAXTON'S PRESS—THE TROY BOOK—THE GAME OF THE CHESS.

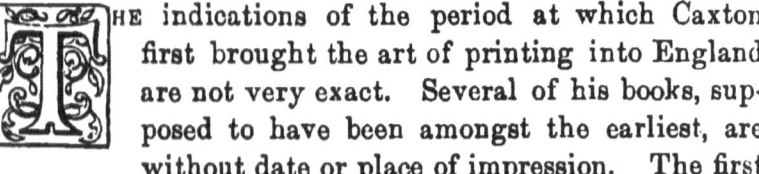HE indications of the period at which Caxton
first brought the art of printing into England
are not very exact. Several of his books, supposed to have been amongst the earliest, are
without date or place of impression. The first
in the title of which a date or a place is mentioned is 'The
Dictes and Sayinges of Philosophres,' translated by the
Earl of Rivers from the French. This bears upon the

title "Enprynted by me William Caxton, at Westminster, the yere of our Lord M.CCCC. lxxvij." Another imprint, three years later, is more precise. It is in the 'Chronicles of Englond,' which book the printer says was "Enprynted by me, William Caxton, in thabbey of Westmynstre by london, &c., the v day of Juyn, the yere of thincarnacion of our lord god M.CCCC. lxxx." In 1485 'A Book of the Noble Hystoryes of Kynge Arthur' was "by me deuyded into xxi bookes chapytred and enprynted and fynysshed, in thabbey Westmestre." The expression "in the Abbey of Westminster" leaves no doubt that beneath the actual roof of some portion of the abbey Caxton carried on his art. Stow, in his 'Survey of London,' says, "In the Eleemosynary or Almonry at Westminster Abbey, now corruptly called the Ambry, for that the alms of the abbey were there distributed to the poor, John Islip, Abbot of Westminster, erected the first press of book-printing that ever was in England, and Caxton was the first that practised it in the said abbey." The careful historian of London here committed one error; John Islip did not become Abbot of Westminster till 1500. John Esteney was made abbot in 1474, and remained such until his death in 1498. His predecessor was Thomas Milling. In Dugdale's 'Monasticon' we find, speaking of Esteney, "It was in this abbot's time, and not in that of Milling, or in that of Abbot Islip, that Caxton exercised the art of printing at Westminster. He is said to have erected his office in one of the side chapels of the abbey, supposed by some of our historians to have been the Ambry or Eleemosynary." Oldys says, "Whoever authorized Caxton, it is certain that he did there, at the entrance of the abbey, exercise the art, from whence a printing-room is to this day called a chapel." When we consider the large extent of building that formed a portion of the abbey of West-

minster, before the house was shorn of its splendour by
Henry the Eighth, we may readily believe that Caxton
might have been accommodated in a less sacred and indeed
less public place than a side chapel of the present church.
There were buildings attached to that church which were
removed to make room for the Chapel of Henry the Seventh.
It has been conjectured that the ancient Scriptorium of
the Abbey, the place where books were transcribed, might
have been assigned to Caxton, to carry on an art which
was fast superseding that of the transcriber. Nor are
there wanting other examples of the encouragement
afforded to printing by great religious societies. As early
as 1480 books were printed at St. Alban's; and in 1525
there was a translation of Boetius printed in the monastery
of Tavistock, by Dan Thomas Richards, monk of the same
monastery. That the intercourse of Caxton with the
Abbot of Westminster was on a familiar footing we learn
from his own statement, in 1490: "My Lord Abbot of
Westminster did shew to me late certain evidences
written in Old English, for to reduce it into our English
now used."

Setting up his press in this sacred place, it is somewhat
remarkable how few of Caxton's books are distinctly of a
religious character.* Not more than five or six can be
held strictly to pertain to theological subjects. Bibles
he could not print, as we shall presently notice.

There is no breviary or book of prayers found to have
issued from his press. The only book distinctly connected
with the Church is 'Liber Festivalis,' or Directions for
keeping Feasts all the year. It is highly probable that
many of such books have perished. But what furnishes
a curious example of the accidents by which the smallest
things may be preserved, there is now existing, preserved

* See the list in Appendix.

in Mr. Douce's collection in the Bodleian Library at Oxford, a handbill, precisely such as a publisher of the present day might distribute, printed in Caxton's largest type, inviting the people to come to his office and buy a certain book regulating the church service. ".If it plese any man spirituel or temporel to bye ony Pyes of two and thre comemoracions of Salisburi vse enprynted after the forme of this present lettre whiche ben wel and truly correct, late hym come to Westmonester into the Almonesryc at the reed pale and he shal have them góod chepe. Supplico stet cedula." The preface to the present Liturgy of the Church of England explains what a Pye was: " The number and hardness of the rules called the Pie, and the manifold changings of the service, was the cause, that to turn the book only was so hard and intricate a matter, that many times there was more business to find out what should be read, than to read it when it was found out." It is a curious fact that printers even at the present day call a confused heap of types Pie ; and whilst no one has attempted to explain the origin of the word, we may venture to suggest that the intricacy of this Romish ordinal might lead the printers to call a mass of confused and deranged letters by a familiar expression of contempt derived from the Pie which they or their predecessors in the art had been accustomed to work upon.

Sir Thomas More has clearly shown the reason why Caxton could not venture to print a Bible, although the people would have greedily bought Wickliff's translation. There were translations of the Bible before Wickliff, and that translation which goes by the name of this great reformer was probably made up in some degree from those previous translations. Wickliff's translation was interdicted, and thus More says, " On account of the penalties ordered by Archbishop Arundel's constitution, though the

old translations that were before Wickliff's days remained
lawful and were in some folk's hands had and read, yet he
thought no printer would lightly be so hot to put any
Bible in print at his own charge—and then hang upon a
doubtful trial whether the first copy of his translation
was made before Wickliff's days or since. For if it were
made since, it must be approved before the printing."
This was a dilemma that Caxton would have been too
prudent to encounter.

In the books printed by Caxton which treat of secular
subjects, there is constant evidence of the sincere and
unpretending piety of this skilful and laborious author
and artisan. He lived in an age when the ancient power
of the church was somewhat waning; and far-sighted
observers saw the cloud no bigger than a man's hand
which indicated the approaching storm. One of his
biographers, the Rev. Mr. Lewis, says of him that "he
expressed a great sense of religion, and wrote like one
who lived in the fear of God, and was very desirous of
promoting his honour and glory." It was in this spirit
that he desired the religious teaching of the people not
to be formal and pedantic. The preface to 'The Doctrinal
of Sapyence,' which was translated out of French into
English by Caxton, contains a curious passage:—" This
that is written in this little book ought the priests to
learn and teach to their parishes : and also it is necessary
for simple priests that understand not the Scriptures : and
it is made for simple people and put in English. And
by cause that for to hear examples stirreth and moveth
the people, that ben simple, more to devotion than to that
great authority of science—as it appeareth by the right
reverend father and doctor Bede, priest, which saith, in
the Histories of England, that a bishop of Scotland, a
subtle and a great clerk, was sent by the clerks of Scot-

land into England for to preach the Word of God; but by cause he used in his sermon subtle authorities, such as [for] simple people had, nor took, no favour, he returned without doing of any great good ne profit, wherefore they sent another of less science: the which was more plain, and used commonly in his sermons examples and parables, by which he profited much more unto the erudition of the simple people than did that other."

But, in wishing the highest knowledge to be simplified and made popular, the good old printer had no thought of rendering knowledge a light and frivolous thing, to be taken up and laid down without earnestness. In his truly beautiful exposition of the uses of knowledge, contained in his prologue to the 'Mirror of the World,' he says, " Let us pray the Maker and Creator of all creatures, God Almighty, that, at the beginning of this book, it list him, of his most bounteous grace, to depart with us of the same that we may learn ; and that learned, to retain ; and that retained, to teach; that we may have so perfect science and knowledge of God, that we may get thereby the health of our souls, and to be partners of his glory, permanent, and without end, in heaven.   Amen."

Gibbon, we think, has taken a somewhat severe view of the character of the works which were produced by the father of English printing:—" It was in the year 1474 that our first press was established in Westminster Abbey, by William Caxton : but in the choice of his authors, that liberal and industrious artist was reduced to comply with the vicious taste of his readers; to gratify the nobles with treatises on heraldry, hawking, and the game of chess, and to amuse the popular credulity with romances of fabulous knights and legends of more fabulous saints."   The historian, however, notices with approbation the laudable desire which Caxton expresses to elucidate the history of

his country. But his censure of the general character
of the works of Caxton's press is somewhat too sweeping.
It appears to us that a more just as well as a more liberal
view of the use and tendency of these works is that of
Thomas Warton, which we may be excused in quoting
somewhat at length :—" By means of French translations,
our countrymen, who understood French much better than
Latin, became acquainted with many useful books which
they would not otherwise have known. With such as-
sistances, a commodious access to the classics was opened,
and the knowledge of ancient literature facilitated and
familiarised in England, at a much earlier period than
is imagined ; and at a time when little more than the
productions of speculative monks and irrefragable doc-
tors could be obtained or were studied. . . . When these
authors, therefore, appeared in a language almost as intelligible as the English, they fell into the hands of
illiterate and common readers, and contributed to sow the
seeds of a national erudition, and to form a popular taste.
Even the French versions of the religious, philosophical,
historical, and allegorical compositions of those more
enlightened Latin writers who flourished in the middle
ages, had their use, till better books came into vogue:
pregnant as they were with absurdities, they communicated instruction on various and new subjects, enlarged
the field of information, and promoted the love of reading,
by gratifying that growing literary curiosity which now
began to want materials for the exercise of its operations. . . . These French versions enabled Caxton, our first
printer, to enrich the state of letters in this country with
many valuable publications. He found it no difficult task,
either by himself or the help of his friends, to turn a considerable number of these pieces into English, which he
printed. Ancient learning had as yet made too little

progress among us to encourage this enterprising and industrious artist to publish the Roman authors in their original language : and had not the French furnished him with these materials, it is not likely that Virgil, Ovid, Cicero, and many other good writers would by the means of his press have been circulated in the English tongue so early as the close of the fifteenth century." Warton adds in a note, " It was a circumstance favourable at least to English literature, owing indeed to the general illiteracy of the times, that our first printers were so little employed on books written in the learned languages. Almost all Caxton's books are English. The multiplication of English copies multiplied English readers, and these again pro-duced new vernacular writers. The existence of a press induced many persons to turn authors who were only qualified to write in their native tongue." Having thus given the somewhat different views of two most able and accomplished scholars, viewing as they did the same objects through different media, we shall proceed to notice some of the more remarkable characteristics of the books issued from Caxton's press, rather regarding them as illus-trations of the state of knowledge and the manners of his time, than as mere bibliographical curiosities.

' The Histories of Troy ' is a book with which our readers must now be tolerably familiar. A writer in the century succeeding Caxton, one Robert Braham, is very severe upon the old printer for this his work : " If a man studious of that history [the Trojan war] should seek to find the same in the doings of William Caxton, in his lewd [idle] ' Recueil of Troye,' what should he then find, think ye? Assuredly none other thing but a long, tedious, and brainless babbling, tending to no end, nor having any certain beginning ; but proceeding therein as an idiot in his folly, that cannot make an end till he be bidden.

Much like the foolish and unsavoury doings of Orestes, whom Juvenal remembereth—which Caxton's ' Recueil,' who so list with judgment peruse, shall rather think his doings worthy to be numbered amongst the trifling tales and barren lewderies of Robin Hood and Bevis of Hampton, than remain as a monument of so worthy an history." We have no sympathy with writers, old or modern, who are severe upon "trifling tales and barren lewderies "— the stories and ballads which are the charm of childhood and the solace of age. It is somewhat hard that Caxton should be thus maltreated for having made the English familiar with that romance of the Trojan war with which all Europe was enamoured in some language or another. The authority which Le Fevre partly followed was the Troy Book of Guido di Colonna ; and he is traced to have translated his book from a Norman-French poet of the time of Edward the Second ; and the Norman is to be traced to Dares Phrygius and Dictys Cretensis, the supposed authors of two ancient works on the History of Troy, but which histories are held to have been manufactured by an Englishman of the twelfth century. Guido di Colonna constructed the most captivating of the romances of chivalry upon these supposititious tales of Troy. Hector and Achilles are surrounded by him with all the attributes of knight-errantry ; and the Grecian manners are Gothicised with all the peculiarities of the civilization of the Middle Ages. Lydgate constructed upon this romance his poem of the Troy Book ; and Chaucer availed himself of it in his poem of 'Troilus and Cressida.' Shakspere, in his wonderful play upon the same part of the Trojan story of the middle ages, has used Chaucer, Lydgate, and Caxton ; and several passages show that our great dramatic poet was perfectly familiar with the translation of our old printer, which was so popular that

by Shakspere's time it had passed through six editions
and continued to be read even in the last century.

'The Book of the whole Life of Jason,' printed by Caxton
in 1475, is another of these middle-age romances, founded
upon the supposititious histories of Dares and Dictys.

Of 'The Game and Play of the Chess,' Caxton printed
two editions, which he translated himself from the French.
The first was finished on the last day of March, 1474; and
it is supposed to have been the first book which he printed
in England.   Bagford says, "Caxton's first book in the
Abbey was 'The Game of Chess;' a book in those times
much in use with all sorts of people, and in all likelihood
first desired by the abbot, and the rest of his friends and
masters."   It was a book that Caxton clearly intended for
the diffusion of knowledge amongst all ranks of people;
for in his second edition he says, in not very complimentary
phrase, "The noble clerks have written and compiled
many notable works and histories," that they might come
"to the knowledge and understanding of such as be
ignorant, of which the number is infinite."   And he adds,
with still plainer speech, that, according to Solomon, "the
number of fools is infinite."   He says that amongst these
noble clerks there was an excellent doctor of divinity in
the kingdom of France, which "hath made a book of the
chess moralised, which at such a time as I was resident in
Bruges came into my hands."   -

It would seem to be an ingenious device of the reverend
writer of the book of chess which Caxton translated, to
associate with very correct instructions as to the mode of
playing the game, such moralisations as would enable him
therewith to teach the people "to understand wisdom and
virtue."   Caxton readily adopts the same notion.   He
dedicates the book to the Duke of Clarence: "Forasmuch
as I have understood and known that you are inclined

unto the commonweal of the king, our said sovereign lord,
his nobles, lords, and common people of his noble realm
of England, and that ye saw gladly the inhabitants of the
same informed in good, virtuous, profitable, and honest
manners." This book contains authorities, sayings, and
stories, "applied unto the morality of the public weal, as
well of the nobles and of the common people, after the
game and play of chess ;" and Caxton trusts that "other,
of what estate or degree he or they stand in, may see in
this little book that they govern themselves as they ought
to do." This book of chess contains four treatises. The
first describes the invention of the game in the time of a
king of Babylon, Emsmerodach, a cruel king, the son of
Nebuchadnezzar, to whom a philosopher showed the game
for the purpose of exhibiting "the manners and condition
of a king, of the nobles, and of the common people and
their offices, and how they should be touched and drawn,
and how he should amend himself and become virtuous."
This is a bold fable, and takes us farther back than Sir
William Jones, who says that chess was imported from
the west of India, in the sixth century, and known imme-
morially in Hindustan by the name of Chaturanga, or the
four members of an army, namely, elephants, horses,
chariots, and foot-soldiers. The second treatise in Caxton's
book describes, first, the office of a king : by this name
the principal piece was always known. Secondly, of the
queen ; this name would seem to belong to the time of
Caxton, for Chaucer and Lydgate call the piece Fers or
Feers, a noble, a general,—hence Peer. Thirdly, of the
Alphyns : this is the same as the present bishop; the
French called this personage the Fou, and Rabelais calls
him the Archer. Fourthly, the knight, who was always
called by this name, in English and French chess. The
rook, the fifth dignified piece, is from the Eastern name

RUC. Caxton goes on to inform us that the third treatise is of the offices of the common people. This treatise relates to the pawns; and a curious thing it is that the eight pawns of the board are taken by him each to represent large classes of the commonalty. The denominations of these classes somewhat vary in the two editions, but their general arrangement is the same. We have, in the first class, labourers and tillers of the earth; in the second, smiths and other workers in iron and metal; in the third, notaries, advocates, scriveners, drapers, and makers of cloth; in the fourth, merchants and changers; in the fifth, physicians, leeches, spicers, and apothecaries; in the sixth, taverners, hostelers, and victuallers; in the seventh, guards of the cities, receivers of custom, and tollers; and lastly, messengers, couriers, ribalds, and players at the dice.

The second edition of 'The Game of the Chess,' which is without date or place, was the first book printed in the English language which contained woodcuts. On the following page we give a fac-simile of the figure of the knight in Caxton's volume.

The original art of engraving on wood, and the production of block-books, gradually merged, as we have seen, into the art of printing from movable types. From that time woodcuts became a secondary part of books, used, indeed, very often by the early printers, but by no means forming an indispensable branch of typography. Imitating the manuscript books, the first printers chiefly employed the wood-engraver upon initial letters; and sometimes the pages of their works were surrounded by borders, which contained white lines or sprigs of foliage upon a black ground. If a figure, or group of figures, was introduced, little more than the outline was first attempted. By degrees, however, endeavours were made to represent gradations of shadow; and a few light hatchings, or white

dots, were employed. All cross-hatchings, such as charac-
terize a line-engraving upon metal, were carefully avoided
by the early woodcutters, on account of the difficulty in
the process. Mr. Ottley, in his 'History of Engraving,'
says that an engraver on wood, of the name of Wohlgemuth (who flourished at Nuremburg about 1480),
"perceived that, though difficult, this was not impossible;"

and, in the cuts of the 'Nuremburg Chronicle,' a "successful attempt was first made to imitate the bold hatchings
of a pen-drawing." Albert Dürer, an artist of extraordinary talent, became the pupil of Wohlgemuth; and
by him, and many others, wood-engraving was carried to
a perfection which it subsequently lost till its revival in
our own country.

Lord Rivers presenting his book to Edward IV.

CHAPTER VII.

FEMALE MANNERS—LORD RIVERS—POPULAR HISTORY—POPULAR SCIENCE
— POPULAR FABLES — POPULAR TRANSLATIONS — THE CANTERBURY
TALES—STATUTES—BOOKS OF CHIVALRY—CAXTON'S LAST DAYS.

N the library belonging to the Archbishops of
Canterbury, at Lambeth, is a beautiful manu-
script, on vellum, of a French work, 'Les Dicts
Moraux des Philosophes,' which contains the
illumination of which the above is a copy.   In
lines written under the illumination the book is stated to
be translated by " Antony erle," by which Lord Rivers is
meant.   This book was printed by Caxton in 1477 ; and
it is held that the man kneeling by the side of the earl in

I

the illumination is the printer of the book. We have already mentioned the confidential intercourse which subsisted between Lord Rivers and his printer, with regard to the revision of this work. (See page 78.) The passages which we there quote are given in a sort of appendix, in which Caxton professes to have himself translated a chapter upon women, which Lord Rivers did not think fit to meddle with, and which he prints with a real or affected apprehension. The printer's statement is altogether such a piece of sly humour, that we willingly transcribe it, trusting that our readers will see the drollery through the quaintness :—

"I find that my said lord hath left out certain and divers conclusions touching women. Whereof I marvelled that my said lord hath not writ on them, nor what hath moved him so to do, nor what cause he had at that time. But I suppose that some fair lady hath desired him to leave it out of his book ; or else he was amorous on some noble lady, for whose love he would not set it in his book ; or else for the very affection, love, and good will that he hath unto all ladies and gentlewomen, he thought that Socrates spared the sooth, and wrote of women more than, truth ; which I cannot think that so true a man and so noble a philosopher as Socrates was, should write otherwise than truth. For if he had made fault in writing of women, he ought not or should not be believed in his other Dictes and Sayings. But I perceive that my said lord knoweth verily that such defaults be not had nor found in the women born and dwelling in these parts nor regions of the world. Socrates was a Greek, born in a far country from hence, which country is all of other conditions than this is, and men and women of other nature than they be here in this country ; for I wot well, of whatsoever condition women be in Greece, the women of this country be

right good, wise, pleasant, humble, discreet, sober, chaste,
obedient to their husbands, true, secret, stedfast, ever busy,
and never idle, attemperate in speaking, and virtuous in
all their works; or at least should be so. For which
causes so evident, my said lord, as I suppose, thought it
was not of necessity to set in his book the sayings of his
author Socrates touching women."

There is a book translated by Caxton from the French,
and printed by him in 1484, which we may incidentally
here notice, as illustrating the female manners of that
century. It is called 'The Knight of the Tower;' and
really would seem to justify the sarcasm of Caxton where
he says, "The women of this country be right good, &c.,
or at least should be so." The preface implies that the
work, though written by a Frenchman, applies to the
contemporary state of society in England; and it may be
well to see how our ladies were employed about four
centuries ago. It appears from this curious performance
that the ladies, although well accomplished in needlework,
confectionery, church music, and even taught something
of the rude surgery of those days, were not great proficients
in reading, and the art of writing was thought to be
better let alone by them. The Knight of the Tower complains of the levity of the ladies. Their extravagance in
dress, the husband's standing complaint, is thus put by
the Knight of the Tower: "The wives say to their
husbands every day, ' Sir, such a wife and such hath such
goodly array that beseemeth her well, and I pray you
I may have of the same.' And if her husband say, ' Wife,
if such have such array, such that are wiser than they
have it not,' she will say, ' No force it is [that is of no
consequence], for they cannot wear it; and if I have it,
ye shall see how well it will become me, for I can wear
it.' And thus with her words her husband must needs

I 2

ordain her that which she desireth, or he shall never have
peace with her, for they will find so many reasons that
they will not be warned [put off]." The women of lower
estate come in for the same censure, the complaint being
that they *fur* their draperies and *fur* their heels. It
appears to have been the practice for ladies to go very
freely to feasts and assemblies, to joustings and tournaments, without what we now call the protection of a
husband or a male relation. A contemporary writer says
they lavished their wealth and corrupted their virtue by
these freedoms. If we may judge from the warnings
which the Knight of the Tower gives his daughters of
the discipline they would receive at the hands of their
husbands for any act of disobedience,—the discipline not
only of hard words, but of harder blows,— it is not to be
wondered at that they sought abroad for some relief to
the gloom and severity of their home lives. It is pleasant,
amidst these illustrations of barbarous and profligate
manners, to find a picture of that real goodness which has
distinguished the female character in all ages, and which,
especially in the times of feudal oppression of which we
are speaking, mitigated the lot of those who were depen-
dent upon the benevolence of the great possessors of
property. The good Lady Cecile of Balleville is thus
described by the Knight of the Tower: "Her daily
ordinance was, that she rose early enough, and had ever
friars and two or three chaplains, which said matins
before her within the oratory. And after, she heard a
high mass and two low, and said her service full devoutly.
And after this she went and arrayed herself, and walked
in her garden or else about her place, saying her other
devotions and prayers. And as time was she went to
dinner. And after dinner, if she wist and know any sick
folk or women in their childbed, she went to see and

visited them, and made to be brought to them her best meat. And there as she might not go herself, she had a servant proper therefore, which rode upon a little horse, and bare with him great plenty of good meat and drink, for to give to the poor and sick folk there as they were. Also she was of such custom, that, if she knew any poor gentlewoman that should be wedded, she arrayed her with her jewels. Also she went to the obsequies of poor gentlewomen, and gave there torches, and such other luminary as it needed thereto. And after she had heard evensong she went to her supper if she fasted not, and timely she went to bed, and made her steward to come to her to wit [know] what meat should be had the next day. She made great abstinence, and wore the hair upon the Wednesday and upon the Friday." This is a true character of the Middle Ages ;—goodness based upon sincere piety, but that degenerating into penances and mortifications, which our Reformed faith teaches us to believe are unnecessary for spiritual elevation.

Caxton's early friend and patron, Lord Rivers, appears, as far as we can judge from the books which remain, to have been the only one of the first English printer's contemporaries who rendered him any literary assistance. He contributed three works to Caxton's press—namely, the ' Dictes and Sayings of the Philosophers,' 'The Moral Proverbs of Christine de Pisa,' and the book named ' Cordial.'

The book named ' Cordial' is clearly described in a prologue by Caxton. It was delivered to him, he says, by Lord Rivers, "for to be imprinted and so multiplied to go abroad among the people, that thereby more surely might be remembered the four last things undoubtedly coming." Caxton, in an elaborate commendation of his patron, of whose former " great tribulation and adversity "

he speaks, says, "It seemeth that he conceiveth well the
mutability and the unstableness of this present life, and
that he desireth, with a great zeal and spiritual love, our
ghostly help and perpetual salvation." Lord Rivers had
indeed borne tribulation since the time when, the flower
of Edward's court, he jousted with the Bastard of Burgundy
in Smithfield, in 1468. In the following year his father
and brother were murdered by a desperate faction at
Northampton. When Lord Rivers, conceiving the mutability and unstableness of life, wrote the book called
' Cordial,' he was only six and thirty years of age. Three
years after Caxton printed the book, the translator was
himself murdered at Pomfret by the Protector Richard.
Shakspere did not do injustice to the noble character of
this peer when he makes him exclaim, when he was led to
the block,

> " Sir Richard Ratcliff, let me tell thee this,—
> To-day shalt thou behold a subject die,
> For truth, for duty, and for loyalty."
> *Richard III.*, Act iii., Scene 2.

There is left to us a remarkable fragment which indi-
cates to us something higher than the ability and literary
attainment of this unfortunate nobleman. It has been
preserved by John Rouse, a contemporary historian, who
lived in the pleasant solitude of Guy's Cliff, near Warwick,
and died there in 1491. He says (we translate from his
Latin), "In the time of his imprisonment at Pomfret he
wrote a balet in English, which has been shown to me,
having these words—Sum what musyng," &c.; and then
Rouse transcribes the ballad, of which the second stanza
is imperfect, but has been supplied from another ancient
copy. Percy, who prints the ballad in his ' Reliques,'
says, "If we consider that it was written during his cruel
confinement in Pomfret Castle, a short time before his

execution in 1483, it gives us a fine picture of the composure and steadiness with which this stout earl beheld his approaching fate." We subjoin the ballad, modernising the orthography :—

> Somewhat musing, and more mourning,
>   In remembering the unstedfastness,
> This world being of such wheeling,
>   Me contrarying what may I guess.
>
> I fear doubtless, remediless
>   Is now to seize my woful chance;
> For unkindness withouten less
>   And no redress, me doth avance,
>
> With displeasance to my grievance
>   And no surance of remedy :
> Lo in this trance, now in substance
>   Such is my dance, willing to die.
>
> Methinks truly bounden am I,
>   And that greatly, to be content,
> Seeing plainly fortune doth wry
>   All contrary from mine intent.
>
> My life was lent me to one intent ;
>   It is nigh spent. Welcome, fortune !
> But I ne went thus to be shent,
>   But she it meant—such is her won [wont].

Turn we to one of the more important works of Caxton, in which he sought to inform his countrymen generally with a knowledge of history. ' The Chronicles of England,' printed in 1480, begins at the fabulous period before the Romans, and ends at the commencement of the reign of Edward IV. The early legends of English History, which even Milton did not disdain to touch upon, are founded upon the ' History ' of Nennius, which was composed in the ninth century, and which was copied by Geoffrey of Monmouth and other of the early chroniclers. Caxton took the thing as he found it, and continued the narrative

to his own time. He deals prudently with contemporary
events. Caxton followed up these chronicles in the same
year with another book, called ' The Description of Britain,'
in which he tells of the extent of the island, its marvels
and wonders, its highways, rivers, cities, and towns, provinces, laws, bishoprics, and languages. He describes also
Scotland and Ireland. Some of his marvels and wonders
are a little astounding; but others are as precise in their
description, and as forcible (brevity being an essential
quality), as we could well desire. Thus of Stonehenge :
" At Stonehinge beside Salisbury there be great stones and
wondrous huge ; and be reared on high, as it were gates
set upon other gates ; nevertheless it is not known cleanly
nor aperceived how and wherefore they be so areared and
so wonderfully hanged."

From the chronicles of his own country Caxton sought
to lead his readers forward to a knowledge of the history
of other countries. He published in 1482 ' The Polychronicon, containing the bearings and deeds of many times.'
This book was originally composed by Higden, a Benedic-
tine monk of Chester; and was translated from Latin into
English by John de Trevisa, who lived in the times of
Edward III. and Richard II. Caxton in his title-page
says, " Imprinted by William Caxton, after having somewhat changed the rude and old English, that is to wit
certain words which in these days be neither used nor
understanden." In another place he says, " And now at
this time simply imprinted and set in form by me, William
Caxton, and a little embellished from the old making."
Caxton was here doing what every person who desires to
advance the knowledge of his time, by extending that
knowledge beyond the narrow circle of scholars and antiquarians, must always do. He popularised an old book ;
he made it intelligible. He did not do,—as some verbal

pedants amongst us still persist in doing,—present our
old writers, and especially our poets, in all the capricious-
ness of their original orthography. He was the first great
diffuser of knowledge amongst us ; and surely we think
he took a judicious course. He says of the 'Polychronicon,' " The book is general, touching shortly many notable
matters." But, *general* as the book was, and extensively
as he desired to circulate it according to his limited means,
he does not approach his task without a due sense of the
importance of the knowledge he was seeking to impart.
The praise of history in his proem is truly eloquent :
" History is a perpetual conservatrice of those things that
have been before this present time ; and also a quotidian
witness of benefits, of malfaits [evil deeds], great acts, and
triumphal victories of all manner of people. And also, if
the terrible feigned fables of poets have much stirred and
moved men to right and conserving of justice, how much
more is to be supposed that history, assertrice of virtue
and a mother of all philosophy, moving our manners to
virtue, reformeth and reconcileth near hand all those men
which through the infirmity of our moral nature hath led
the most part of their life in otiosity [idleness], and mis-
spended their time, passed right soon out of remembrance :
of which life and death is equal oblivion." Again, " Other
monuments distributed in divers changes endure but for
a short time or season ; but the virtue of history diffused
and spread by the universal world hath time, which con-
sumeth all other things, as conservatrice and keeper of her
work."

' The Image or Mirror of the World ' is one of the popular
books which Caxton translated from the French. It treats
of a vast variety of subjects, after the imperfect natural
philosophy of those days. We have an account of the
seven liberal arts; of nature, how she worketh ; and how

the earth holdeth him right in the middle of the world.
We have also much geographical information, amongst
which the wonders of Inde occupy a considerable space.
Meteorology and astronomy take up another large portion.
The work concludes with an account of the celestial
paradise. This book seems specially addressed to high and
courtly readers, for Caxton says, 'The hearts of nobles, in
eschewing of idleness at such time as they have none other
virtuous occupations on hand, ought to exercise them in
reading, studying, and visiting the noble feats and deeds
of the sage and wise men, sometime travelling in profitable
virtues; of whom it happeneth oft that some be inclined
to visit the books treating of sciences particular; and
other to read and visit books speaking of feats of arms, of
love, or of other marvellous histories; and among all other,
this present book, which is called the 'Image or Mirror
of the World,' ought to be visited, read, and known, by
cause it treateth of the world, and of the wonderful division thereof." But the translator tells us, "I have en-
deavoured me therein, at the request and desire, cost and
dispense, of the honourable and worshipful man, Hugh
Brice, citizen and alderman of London." We may therefore believe that Caxton intended this book for a wider
circulation than that of the nobles whom he addresses;
especially as he says, "I have made it so plain that every
man reasonable may understand it, if he advisedly and
attentively read it, or hear it." The good old printer
rendered the book intelligible to all classes, under the
condition that all who read it should give their attention.
This is one of the books into which Caxton has introduced
woodcuts, giving twenty-seven figures, "without which it
may not lightly [easily] be understood." These twenty-
seven figures are diagrams, explanatory of some of the
scientific principles laid down in this book; but there are

eleven other cuts illustrative of other subjects treated in
the work. An idea may be formed of the manner in which
those cuts are engraved from the following fac-simile of
' Music.'

One of the most popular books of Caxton's translation
must unquestionably have been the ' History of Reynard the
Fox.' It is held that this work was composed in the twelfth
century ; and surely the author must have been a man of
high genius to have constructed a fable which has been ever
since popular in all countries, and delights us even to this
hour. Caxton has no woodcuts to his edition, to which the
book subsequently owed a portion of its attractions.

' The Subtil Histories and Fables of Esop,' translated by
Caxton from the French, were printed by him in 1483,
" The first year of the reign of King Richard the Third."

In the first leaf there is a supposed portrait of Esop, a large rough woodcut, exhibiting him as he is described, with a great head, large visage, long jaws, sharp eyes, a short neck, *curb*-backed, and so forth. There is a controversy whether Richard the Third was a deformed man or not. It is held by many that it was one of the scandals put forth under his triumphant successor (which scandal Shakspere has for ever made current), that Richard was

> " Cheated of feature by dissembling nature,
> Deform'd, unfinish'd."

It strikes us that Caxton would scarcely have ventured, in the first year of King Richard III., to exhibit a print of a hump-backed Esop (for any print was then a rare thing), if his dread sovereign had been remarkable amongst the people for a similar defect. The conclusion of these fables of Esop has a story told by Caxton as from himself, which is a remarkable specimen of a plain narrative style, with a good deal of sly humour :—

" Now then I will finish all these fables with this tale that followeth, which a worshipful priest and a parson told me late : he said that there were dwelling at Oxenford two priests, both Masters of Arts—of whom that one was quick and could put himself forth ; and that other was a good simple priest. And so it happened that the master that was pert and quick was anon promoted to a benefice or twain, and after to prebends, and for to be a dean of a great prince's chapel, supposing and weening that his fellow, the simple priest, should never be promoted, but be always an annual, or, at the most, a parish priest. So after a long time that this worshipful man, this dean, came running into a good parish with five or seven horses, like a prelate, and came into the church of the said parish, and found there this good simple man, sometime his fellow,

which came and welcomed him lowly. And that other
bade him 'Good morrow, Master John,' and took him
slightly by the hand, and axed him where he dwelt. And
the good man said, ' In this parish.'   ' How,' said he, ' are
ye here a sole priest, or a parish priest?' ' Nay, sir,' said
he, ' for lack of a better, though I am not able nor worthy,
I am parson and curate of this parish.' And then that
other vailed [lowered] his bonnet, and said, ' Master Parson,
I pray you to be not displeased ; I had supposed ye had
not been beneficed. But, master,' said he, ' I pray you
what is this benefice worth to you a year?' ' Forsooth,'
said the good simple man, ' I wot never ; for I make never
accompts thereof, how well I have had it four or five
years.' ' And know ye not,' said he, ' what it is worth?—
it should seem a good benefice.' ' No, forsooth,' said he,
' but I wot well what it shall be worth to me.'   ' Why,
said he, ' what shall it be worth?' ' Forsooth,' said he,
' if I do my true dealing in the cure of my parishes in
preaching and teaching, and do my part belonging to my
cure, I shall have heaven therefore. And if their souls be
lost, or any of them, by my default, I shall be punished
therefore. And hereof I am sure.' And with that word
the rich dean was abashed : and thought he should be the
better, and take more heed to his cures and benefices than
he had done. This was a good answer of a good priest
and an honest. And herewith I finish this book, translated
and imprinted by me, William Caxton." The moral of the
fable is not obsolete.

Ono of Caxton's most splendid books, of which he seems
to have printed three editions, was ' The Golden Legend.'
This is, indeed, an important work, printed in double
columns, and containing between four and five hundred
pages, which are largely illustrated with woodcuts. It was
not without great caution, as we have already mentioned

(page 98), that Caxton proceeded with this heavy and expensive undertaking. Happy would it have been for all printers if puissant and virtuous earls, and others in high places had thought it a duty to encourage knowledge by taking a "reasonable quantity" of a great work; but happier are we now, when, such assistance being grudgingly bestowed or honestly despised, the makers of books can depend upon something more satisfying than the rich man's purse, which was generally associated with "the proud man's contumely."

In the prologue to the 'Golden Legend' Caxton recites several of the works which he had previously "translated out of French into English at the request of certain lords, ladies, and gentlemen." Those recited are the 'Recueil of Troy,' the 'Book of the Chess,' 'Jason,' the 'Mirror of the World,' Ovid's 'Metamorphoses,' and 'Godfrey of Boulogne.' It is remarkable that no printed copy exists of Ovid's 'Metamorphoses;' but in the library of Magdalen College, Cambridge, there is a manuscript containing five books of the 'Metamorphoses,' which purport to be translated by Caxton. It was evidently a part of his plan for the encouragement of liberal education, to present a portion of the people with translations of the classics through the ready means that were open to him of re-translation from the French. Many translators in later times have availed themselves of such aids, without the honesty to indicate the immediate sources of their versions. Caxton printed 'The Book of Tully of Old Age,' and 'Tullius his Book of Friendship.' He seems to have had great difficulty in obtaining a copy of an old translation of 'Tullius de Senectute.' The Book 'De Amicitia' was translated by John, Earl of Worcester, the celebrated adherent of the house of York, who was beheaded in 1470. Caxton, we think somewhat unnecessarily, limits the perusal of the treatise on

Old Age. "This book is not requisite nor eke convenient for every rude and simple man, which understandeth not of science nor cunning, and for such as have not heard of the noble policy and prudence of the Romans; but for noble, wise, and great lords, gentlemen, and merchants, that have been and daily be occupied in matter touching the public weal: and in especial unto them that been passed their green age, and eke their middle age, called virility, and been approached unto *senectute*, called old and ancient age. Wherein they may see how to suffer and bear the same patiently; and what surety and virtue been in the same, and have also cause to be joyous and glad that they have escaped and passed the manifold perils and doubteous adventures that been in juvente and youth, as in this said book here following ye may more plainly see."

'The Book of Eneydos,' compiled from Virgil, is not a translation of Virgil's great epic, but a sort of historical narrative formed upon the course of the poet's great story. The most remarkable passage of this book is that of Caxton's preface, in which he complains of the unsteadfastness of our language, and the difficulty that he found between plain, rude, and curious terms. (See page 15.) In this translation he again limits his work to a particular class of persons; as if he felt, which was probably a prejudice of his time, that the inferior members of the laity ought not to touch anything that pertained to scholastic learning. He says, "Forasmuch as this present book is not for a rude uplandish man to labour therein, nor read it, but only for a clerk and a noble gentleman that feeleth and understandeth in faits of arms, in love, and in noble chivalry: therefore, in mean between both, I have reduced and translated this said book into our English, not over rude nor curious, but in such terms as shall be understanden, by God's grace, according to my copy."

'The book called Cathon' (Cato's Morals) was destined by
Caxton for a wider circulation:—"In my judgment it is
the best book for to be taught to young children in schools,
and also to people of every age it is full convenient if it be
well understanden."

Dr. Dibdin, in his 'Typographical Antiquities,' says
of Caxton, " Exclusively of the labours attached to the
working of his press as a new art, our typographer con-
trived, though well stricken in years, to translate not
fewer than five thousand closely printed folio pages. As
a translator, therefore, he ranks among the most laborious,
and, I would hope, not the least successful, of his tribe.
The foregoing conclusion is the result of a careful enumeration of all the books translated as well as printed by
him; which [the translated books], if published in the
modern fashion, would extend to nearly twenty-five octavo
volumes!" The exact nature of his labours seems, as
might well be imagined, to have been often determined by
very accidental circumstances. One noble lord requests
him to produce this book, and one worshipful gentleman
urges him to translate that. He says himself of his Virgil,
" After divers works made, translated, and achieved, having
no work in hand, I, sitting in my study whereas lay many
divers pamphlets and books, happened that to my hand
came a little book in French, which late was translated out
of Latin by some noble clerk of France, which book is
named Eneydos, made in Latin by that noble poet and
great clerk Virgil." Some books, indeed, he would be
determined to print by their existing popularity. Such
were his two editions of Chaucer's ' Canterbury Tales,'
which we may be sure, from his sound criticism, he felt
the necessity of promulgating to a much wider circle than
had been reached by the transcribers. (See page 36.)
Caxton was especially the devoted printer of Chaucer.

His truly honourable conduct in venturing upon a new
edition of the 'Canterbury Tales,' when he found his first
was incorrect, exhibits an example in the first printer and
the first publisher which the printers and publishers of all
subsequent times ought to reverence and imitate. The
early printers, English and foreign, were indeed a high
and noble race. They did not set themselves up to be the
patrons of letters; they did not dispense their dole to
scholars grudgingly and thanklessly; they worked with
them; they encountered with them the risks of profit and
of fame; they were scholars themselves; they felt the
deep responsibility of their office; they carried on the
highest of all commerce in an elevated temper; they were
not mere hucksters and chafferers. It was in no spirit of
pride, it was in the spirit of duty, that Caxton raised a
table of verses to Chaucer in Westminster Abbey. In his
edition of Boetius, which he gives us to understand was
translated by Master Geoffrey Chaucer, he says, " And
furthermore I desire and require you, that of your charity
ye would pray for the soul of the said worshipful man
Geoffrey Chaucer, first translator of this said book into
English, and embellisher in making the said language
ornate and fair, which shall endure perpetually, and therefore he ought eternally to be remembered; of whom the
body and corps lieth buried in the Abbey of Westminster,
beside London, to fore the chapel of Saint Benet, by whose
sepulture is written on a table, hanging on a pillar, his
epitaph made by a poet-laureate, whereof the copy
followeth." The writer of the Life of Chaucer, in the
' Biographia Britannica,' says, " It is very probable he lay
beneath a large stone of gray marble in the pavement
where the monument to Mr. Dryden now stands, which is
in the front of that chapel [St. Benet's], upon the erecting
of which [Dryden's monument] this stone was taken up,

K

and sawed in pieces to make good the pavement. At least
this seems best to answer the description of the place
given by Caxton." There appears, according to the
ancient editors of Chaucer's works, to have been two
Latin lines upon his tombstone previous to the epitaph set
up upon a pillar by Caxton. That epitaph was written
by Stephanus Suriganius, poet-laureate of Milan. The
monument of Chaucer, which still remains in the Abbey,
around which the ashes of Spenser, and Beaumont, and
Drayton, and Jonson, and Cowley, and Dryden have
clustered, was erected by an Oxford student in 1555.
There might have been worse things preserved, and yet to
be looked upon, in that Abbey, than honest old Caxton's
epitaph upon him whom he calls "the worshipful father
and first founder and embellisher of ornate eloquence in
our English."

As the popularity of Chaucer demanded various impressions of his works from Caxton's press, so did he print
an apparently cheap edition of Gower's 'Confessio Amantis,'
in small type. Two of Lydgate's works were also printed
by him. The more fugitive poetry which issued from his
press has probably all perished. In one of the volumes of
Old Ballads in the British Museum is a fragment of a
poem, of which nothing further is known, telling the
story of some heroine that lived a life of unvaried
solitude :—

> "From her childhood I find that she fled
>   Office of woman, and to wood she went,
> And many a wild harte's blood she shed
>   With arrows broad that she to them sent."

One of the most important uses of early printing in
England is to be found in fragments of the Statutes of the
Realm, made in the first parliament of Richard III., and
in the first, second, and third parliaments of Henry VII.,

some leaves of which exist. That the promulgation of the laws would soon follow the introduction of the art of printing was a natural consequence. Early in the next century the publication of Acts of Parliament became an important branch of trade; and a King's Printer was formally appointed. Up to our own times all the cheapening processes of the art of printing had been withheld, at least in their results, from that branch of printing which was to instruct the people in their new laws. The Statutes were the dearest of books, and kept dear for no other purpose but to preserve one relic of the monopolies of the days of the Stuarts. The abuse has been partially remedied.

We have purposely reserved to the conclusion of this account of the productions of Caxton's press, some notice of those works to the undertaking of which he seems to have been moved by his familiarity with the frequenters of the court,—those whose talk was of tournaments and battles, of gallant knights and noble dames; and whose heads, like that of the worthy Knight of La Mancha, were "full of nothing but enchantments, quarrels, battles, challenges, wounds, complaints, amours, torments." It is quite marvellous to look upon the enthusiasm with which Master Caxton deals with these matters in the days when he had achieved

"The silver livery of advised age."

It offers us one of the many proofs of the energy and youthfulness of his character. We have already quoted his address to the knights of England (see page 66), given in his 'Book of the Order of Chivalry,' supposed to have been printed in 1484. After this address he proposes a question which shows that he considers he has fallen upon degenerate days. "How many knights be there now in

England that have the use and the exercise of a knight?
that is to wit, that he knoweth his horse, and his horse
him ; that is to say, he being ready at a point to have all
thing that belongeth to a knight, an horse that is according
and broken after his hand, his armour and harness suit,
and so forth, et cetera. I suppose, an a due search should
be made, there should be many founden that lack: the
more pity is! I would it pleased our sovereign Lord, that
twice or thrice a year, or at the least once, he would cry
jousts of peace, to the end that every knight should have
horse and harness, and also the use and craft of a knight,
and also to tourney one against one, or two against two ;
and the best to have a prize, a diamond or jewel, such as
should please the prince. This should cause gentlemen to
resort to the ancient customs of chivalry to great fame
and renown: and also to be alway ready to serve their
prince when he shall call them, or have need." There is
always some compensating principle arising in the world
to prevent its too rapid degeneracy ; and thus, although
the tournament has long ceased, except as a farce, there is
many a noble who may still say, " That he knoweth his
horse, and his horse him," through the attractions of
Melton Mowbray and Epsom. Hunting and horse-racing
have done much to keep up our pristine civilization. In
' The Fait of Arms and Chivalry,' 1489, Caxton undertakes
a higher strain. He translates this book, " to the end that
every gentleman born to arms and all manner men of war,
captains, soldiers, victuallers, and all other, should have
knowledge how they ought to behave them in the faits of
war and of battles." And yet, strange to relate, this
belligerent book was written by a fair lady, Christina of
Pisa. The ' Histories of King Arthur,' printed in 1485,
lands us at once into all the legendary hero-worship of the
Middle Ages. Caxton, in his preface to this translation by

Sir Thomas Mallory, gives us a pretty full account of the Nine Worthies, "the best that ever were;" and then he goes on to expound his reasons for once doubting whether the Histories of Arthur were anything but fables, and how he was convinced that he was a real man. But surely in these chivalrous books Caxton had an honest purpose. He exhorts noble lords and ladies, with all other estates, to read this said book, "wherein they shall well find many joyous and pleasant histories, and noble and renowned acts of humanity, gentleness, and chivalries; for herein may be seen noble chivalry, courtesy, humanity, friendliness, hardiness, love, friendship, cowardice, murder, hate, virtue, and sin. Do after the good, and leave the evil, and it shall bring you to good fame and renown." ' The Life of Charles the Great ' succeeded the ' Histories of King Arthur;' for, according to Caxton, Charlemagne was the second of the three worthy. It is in the preface to this book that Caxton says that his father and mother in his youth sent him to school, by which, by the sufferance of God, he gets his living.

We may conclude this imperfect description of Caxton's labours in the literature of romance and chivalry, so characteristic of the age in which he lived, with the following extract from the ' History of King Blanchardine and Queen Eglantine his Wife,' which he translated from the French, at the command of the Duchess of Somerset, mother of King Henry VII. The passage shows us that the old printers were dealers in foreign books as well as in their own productions: " Which book I had long to fore *sold* to my said lady, and knew well that the story of it was honest and joyful to all virtuous young noble gentlemen and women, for to read therein, as for their pastime. For under correction, in my judgment, histories of noble feats and valiant acts of arms and war, which have been

achieved in old time of many noble princes, lords, and
knights, are as well for to see and know their valiantness
for to stand in the special grace and love of their ladies,
and in like wise for gentle young ladies and demoiselles
for to learn to be stedfast and constant in their part to
them that they once have promised and agreed to, such as
have put their lives oft in jeopardy for to please them to
stand in grace, as it is to occupy the ken and study over-
much in books of contemplation." This is a defence of
novel-reading which we could scarcely have expected at
so early a period of our literature.

In 1490 Caxton was approaching, according to all his
biographers, to the great age of fourscore. About this
period he appears to have consigned some relation to the
grave, perhaps his wife. In the first year of the churchwardens' accounts of the parish of St. Margaret's, Westminster, from May 17, 1490, to June 3, 1492, there is the
following entry :—

"Item; atte bureynge of Mawde Caxton for
    torches and tapers . . . . iiij' ij⁴."

On the 15th June, 1490, Caxton finished translating out
of French into English 'The Art and Craft to know well
to die.' The commencement of the book is an abrupt one :
"When it is so, that what man maketh or doeth it is
made to come to some end, and if the thing be good and
well made it must needs come to good end; then by
better and greater reason every man ought to intend in
such wise to live in this world, in keeping the command-
ments of God, that he may come to a good end. And then
out of this world, full of wretchedness and tribulations,
he may go to heaven unto God and his saints, unto joy
perdurable."

That the end of Caxton was a good end we have little doubt. We have a testimony, which we shall presently see, that he *worked* to the end. He worked upon a book of pious instruction to the last day of his life. He was not slumbering when his call came. He was still labouring at the work for which he was born.

There is the following entry in the churchwardens' accounts of the parish of St. Margaret, in the second year of the period we have above mentioned :—

"Item; atte bureyng of WILLIAM CAXTON
for iiij torches . . . . vj^s viii^d
Item; for the belle at same bureyng . vj^d."

Mark of Wynkyn de Worde.*

CHAPTER VIII.

THE CHAPEL—THE COMPANIONS—INCREASE OF READERS—BOOKS MAKE
READERS—CAXTON'S TYPES—WYNKYN'S DREAM—THE FIRST PAPER-
MILL.

r was evensong time when, after a day of listless-
ness, the printers in the Almonry at West-
minster prepared to close the doors of their
workshop. This was a tolerably spacious
room, with a carved oaken roof. The setting sun shone
brightly into the chamber, and lighted up such furniture
as no other room in London could then exhibit. Between
the columns which supported the roof stood two presses
—ponderous machines. A *form* of types lay unread upon
the *table* of one of these presses; the other was empty.
There were *cases* ranged between the opposite columns;
but there was no *copy* suspended ready for the compositors

* He always, in these marks, associated the device of Caxton with
his own ; glorying, as he well might, in succeeding to the business of
his honoured master, and continuing for so many years the good work
which he had begun.

to proceed with in the morning. No heap of wet paper was piled upon the floor. The *balls*, removed from the presses, were rotting in a corner. The *ink-blocks* were dusty, and a thin film had formed over the oily pigment. He who had set these machines in motion, and filled the whole space with the activity of mind, was dead. His daily work was ended.

Three grave-looking men, decently clothed in black, were girding on their swords. Their caps were in their hands. The door opened, and the chief of the workmen came in. It was Wynkyn de Worde. With short speech, but with looks of deep significance, he called a *chapel*—the printer's parliament—a conclave as solemn and as omnipotent as the Saxons' Witenagemot. Wynkyn was the Father of the Chapel.

The four drew their high stools round the *imposing-stone* —those stools on which they had sat through many a day of quiet labour, steadily working to the distant end of some ponderous folio, without hurry or anxiety. Upon the stone lay two uncorrected folio pages—a portion of the 'Lives of the Fathers.' The *proof* was not returned. He that they had followed a few days before to his grave in Saint Margaret's Church had lifted it once back to his failing eyes,—and then they closed in night.

"Companions," said Wynkyn (surely that word "*companions*" tells of the antiquity of printing, and of the old love and fellowship that subsisted amongst its craft)·— "companions, the good work will not stop."

"Wynkyn," said Richard Pynson, "who is to carry on the work?"

"I am ready," answered Wynkyn.

A faint expression of joy rose to the lips of these honest men, but it was damped by the remembrance of him they had lost.

" He died," said Wynkyn, " as he lived. The ' Lives of
the Holy Fathers' is finished, as far as the translator's
labour. There is the rest of the copy. Read the words
of the last page, which *I* have written :—

" Thus endeth the most virtuous history of the devout
and right-renowned lives of holy fathers, living in desert,
worthy of remembrance to all well-disposed persons,
which hath been translated out of French into English by
William Caxton of Westminster, late dead, and finished
at the last day of his life."*

The tears were in all their eyes; and "God rest his
soul!" was whispered around.

"Companion," said William Machlinia, "is not this a
hazardous enterprise?".

" I have encouragement," replied Wynkyn; "the
Lady Margaret, his Highness' mother, gives me aid. So
droop not, fear not. We will carry on the work briskly
in our good master's house.—So fill the case."†

A shout almost mounted to the roof.

"But why should we fear? You, Machlinia, you,
Lettou, and you, dear Richard Pynson, if you choose not
to abide with your old companion here, there is work for
you all in these good towns of Westminster, London, and
Southwark. You have money; you know where to buy
types. Printing *must* go forward."

"Always full of heart," said Pynson. "But you forget
the statute of King Richard; we cannot say ' God rest
his soul,' for our old master scarcely ever forgave him
putting Lord Rivers to death. You forget the statute.
We ought to know it, for we printed it. I can turn to

---

* These are the words with which this book closes.
† "Wynkyn de Worde this hath set in print,
    In William Caxton's house :—so fill the case."
                        Stanzas to ' Scala Perfectionis,' 1494.

the file in a moment. It is the Act touching the merchants of Italy, which forbids them selling their wares in this realm. Here it is: 'Provided always that this Act, or any part thereof, in no wise extend or be prejudicial of any let, hurt, or impediment to any artificer or merchant stranger, of what nation or country he be or shall be of, for bringing into this realm, or selling by retail or otherwise, of any manner of books written or imprinted.' Can we stand up against that, if we have more presses than the old press of the Abbey of Westminster?"

"Ay, truly, we can, good friend," briskly answered Wynkyn. "Have we any books in our stores? Could we ever print books fast enough? Are there not readers rising up on all sides? Do we depend upon the court? The mercers and the drapers, the grocers and the spicers of the city, crowd here for our books. The rude uplandish men even take our books; they that our good master rather vilipended. The tapsters and taverners have our books. The whole country-side cries out for our ballads and our Robin Hood stories; and, to say the truth, the citizen's wife is as much taken with our King Arthurs and King Blanchardines as the most noble knight that Master Caxton ever desired to look upon in his green days of jousts in Burgundy. So fill the case."*

"But if foreigners bring books into England," said cautious William Machlinia, "there will be more books than readers."

"Books make readers," rejoined Wynkyn. "Do you remember how timidly even our bold master went on before he was safe in his sell? Do you forget how he asked this

---

* To "fill the case" is to put fresh types in the case, ready to arrange in new pages. The bibliographers scarcely understood the technical expression of honest Wynkyn.

lord to take a copy, and that knight to give him something in fee; and how he bargained for his summer venison and his winter venison, as an encouragement in his ventures? But he found a larger market than he ever counted upon, and so shall we all. Go ye forth, my brave fellows. Stay not to work for me, if you can work better for yourselves. · I fear no rivals."

"Why, Wynkyn," interposed Pynson, "you talk as if printing were as necessary as air; books as food, or clothing, or fire."

"And so they will be some day. What is to stop the want of books? Will one man have the command of books, and another desire them not? The time may come when every man shall require books."

"Perhaps," said Lettou, who had an eye to printing the Statutes, "the time may come when every man shall want to read an Act of Parliament, instead of the few lawyers who buy our Acts now."

"Hardly so," grunted Wynkyn.

"Or perchance you think that, when our sovereign liege meets his Peers and Commons in Parliament, it were well to print a book some month or two after, to tell what the said Parliament said, as well as ordained?"

"Nay, nay, you run me hard," said Wynkyn.

"And if within a month, why not within a day? Why shouldn't we print the words as fast as they are spoken? We only want fairy fingers to pick up our types, and presses that Doctor Faustus and his devils may some day make, to tell all London to-morrow morning what is done this morning in the palace at Westminster."

"Prithee, be serious," ejaculated Wynkyn. "Why do you talk such gallymaufry? I was speaking of possible things; and I really think the day may come when one person in a thousand may read books and buy books, and we shall have a trade almost as good as that of armourers and fletchers."

"The Bible!" exclaimed Pynson; "O that we might print the Bible! I know of a copy of Wickliffe's Bible. That were indeed a book to print!"

"I have no doubt, Richard," replied Wynkyn, "that the happy time may come when a Bible shall be chained in every church, for every Christian man to look upon. You remember when our brother Hunte showed us the chained books in the Library at Oxford. So a century or two hence a Bible may be found in every parish. Twelve thousand parishes in England? We should want more paper in that good day, Master Richard."

"You had better fancy at once," said Lettou, "that every housekeeper will want a Bible! Heaven save the mark, how some men's imaginations run away with them!"

"I cannot see," interposed Machlinia, "how we can venture upon more presses in London. Here are two. They have been worked well, since the day when they were shipped at Cologne. Here are five good founts of type, as much as a thousand weight—*Great Primer, Double Pica, Pica*—a large and a small face, and *Long Primer*. They have well worked; they are pretty nigh worn out. What man would risk such an adventure, after our good old master? He was a favourite at court and in cloister. He was well patronized   Who is to patronize us?"

"The people, I tell you," exclaimed Wynkyn. "The babe in the cradle wants an Absey-book; the maid at her distaff wants a ballad; the priest wants his Pie; the young lover wants a romance of chivalry to read to his mistress; the lawyer wants his Statutes; the scholar wants his Virgil and Cicero. They will all want more the more they are supplied. How many in England have a book at all, think you? Let us make books cheaper by

To the right noble/right excellent & vertuous prince
George duc of Clarence Erle of warwyk and of
Salisbury/grete Chamberlayn of Englond & Leutenant
of Irelond oldest Broder of kynge Edwarde by the grace
of god kynge of Englond and of fraunce/your most
humble seruant william Caxton amonge other of your
seruantes sendes vnto your peas. helthe. Joye and victo-
rye vpon your Enemyes /

Caxton's Type.

printing more of them at once. The churchwardens of
St. Margaret's asked me six-and-eightpence yesterday for
the volume that our master left the parish ;* for not a
copy can I get, if we should want to print again. Six-
and-eightpence! That was exactly what he charged his
customers for the volume. Print five hundred instead of
two hundred, and we could sell it for three-and-four-
pence."

"And ruin ourselves," said Machlinia. "Master
Wynkyn, I shall fear to work for you if you go on so
madly. What has turned your head ?"

"Hearken," said Wynkyn. "The day our good master
was buried I had no stomach for my home. I could not
eat. I could scarcely look on the sunshine. There was a
chill at my heart. I took the key of our office, for you all
were absent, and I came here in the deep twilight. I sat
down in Master Caxton's chair. I sat till I fancied I saw
him moving about, as he was wont to move, in his furred ·
gown, explaining this copy to one of us, and shaking his
head at that proof to the other. I fell asleep. Then I
dreamed a dream, a wild dream, but one that seems to
have given me hope and courage. There I sat, in the old
desk at the head of this room, straining my eyes at the old
proofs. The room gradually expanded. The four *frames*
went on multiplying, till they became innumerable. I
saw *case* piled upon *case;* and *form* side by side with *form*.
All was bustle, and yet quiet, in that room. Readers
passed to and fro; there was a glare of many lights; all
seemed employed in producing one folio, an enormous
folio. In an instant the room had changed. I heard a
noise as of many wheels. I saw sheets of paper covered

* There is a record in the parish books of St. Margaret's of the
churchwardens selling for 6s. 8d. one of the books bequeathed to
the church by William Caxton.

with ink as quickly as I pick up this type. Sheet upon
sheet, hundreds of sheets, thousands of sheets, came from
forth the wheels—flowing in unstained, like corn from the
hopper, and coming out printed, like flour to the sack.
They flew abroad as if carried over the earth by the winds.
Again the scene changed. In a cottage, an artificer's
cottage, though it had many things in it which belong to
princes' palaces, I saw a man lay down his basket of tools
and take up one of these sheets. He read it; he laughed,
he looked angry; tears rose to his eyes; and then he read
aloud to his wife and children. I asked him to show me
the sheet. It was wet; it contained as many types as our
'Mirror of the World.' But it bore the date of 1844. I
looked around, and I saw shelves of books against that
cottage wall—large volumes and small volumes; and a boy
opened one of the large volumes and showed me number-
less block-cuts; and the artificer and his wife and his
children gathered round me, all looking with glee towards
their books, and the good man pointed to an inscription on
his book-shelves, and I read these words,

MY LIBRARY A DUKEDOM.

I woke in haste; and, whether awake or dreaming I know
not, my master stood beside me, and smilingly exclaimed,
'This is my fruit.' I have encouragement in this
dream."

  " Friend Wynkyn," said Pynson, " these are distempered
visions. The press may go forward; I think it will go
forward. But I am of the belief that the press will never
work but for the great and the learned, to any purpose
of profit to the printer. How can we ever hope to send
our wares abroad? We may hawk our ballads and our
merry jests through London ; but the citizens are too busy

to heed them, and the apprentices and serving-men too
poor to buy them. To the country we cannot send them.
Good lack, imagine the poor pedlar tramping with a pack
of books to Bristol or Winchester! Before he could reach
either city through our wild roads, he would have his
throat cut or be starved. Master Wynkyn, we shall always
have a narrow market till the king mends his highways,
and that will never be."

"I am rather for trying, Master Wynkyn," said Lettou,
"some good cutting jest against our friends in the Abbey,
such as Dan Chaucer expounded touching the friars. That
would sell in these precincts."

"Hush!" exclaimed Wynkyn: "the good fathers are
our friends; and though some murmur against them, we
might have worse masters."

"I wish they would let us print the Bible though,"
ejaculated Pynson.

"The time will come, and that right soon," exclaimed
the hopeful Wynkyn.

"So be it," said they one and all.

"But what fair sheet of paper is that in your hand,
good Wynkyn?" said Pynson.

"Master Richard, we are all moving onward. This is
English-made paper. Is it not better than the brown
thick paper we have had from over the sea? How *he*
would have rejoiced in this accomplishment of John Tate's
longing trials! Ay, Master Richard, this fair sheet was
made in the new mill at Hertford; and well am I minded
to use it in our Bartholomæus, which I shall straightly
put in hand, when the Formschneider is ready. I have
thought anent it; I have resolved on it; and I have in-
dited some rude verses touching the matter, simple person
as I am :—

"For in this world to reckon every thing
  Pleasure to man, there is none comparable
As is to read and understanding
  In books of wisdom—they ben so delectable,
  Which sound to virtue, and ben profitable;
And all that love such virtue ben full glad
Books to renew, and cause them to be made.

And also of your charity call to remembrance
  The soul of William Caxton, first printer of this book
In Latin tongue at Cologne, himself to advance,
  That every well-disposed man may thereon look;
  And John Tate the younger joy mote [may] he brook,
Which hath late in England made this paper thin,
That now in our English this book is printed in."

"Fairly rhymed, Wynkyn," said Lettou. "But John
Tate the younger is a bold fellow. Of a surety England
can never support a paper-mill of its own."

"Come, to business," said William of Mechlin.

providence of God) the method of cutting (*incidendi*) the characters
in a matrix, that the letters might each be singly cast, instead of
being cut. He privately cut matrices for the whole alphabet; and
when he showed his master the letters cast from these matrices,
Fust was so pleased with the contrivance, that he promised Peter to
give him his only daughter Christina in marriage ; a promise which
he soon after performed. But there were as many difficulties at first
with these letters as there had been before with wooden ones ; the
metal being too soft to support the force of the impression : but this
defect was soon remedied by mixing the metal with a substance
which sufficiently hardened it." John Schoeffer, the son of Peter,
who was also a printer, confirms this account, adding, "Fust and
Schoeffer concealed this new improvement by administering an
oath of secrecy to all whom they intrusted, till the year 1462, when,
by the dispersion of their servants into different countries, at the
sacking of Mentz by the Archbishop Adolphus, the invention was
publicly divulged."

APPENDIX B.

BOOKS PRINTED BY CAXTON.

To our first printer are assigned 64 works, from 1471 to 1491. We subjoin a list of them, furnished to the ' Penny Cyclopædia ' by Sir Henry Ellis, Principal Librarian of the British Museum. In this list are included the French edition of the ' Recueil,' and the Oration of Russell, which are considered doubtful.

1. 'Le Recueil des Histoires de Troyes, compose par raoulle le feure, chapellein de Monseigneur le duc Philippe de Bourgoingne en l'an de grace mil cccclxiiii.,' fol.

2. ' Propositio clarissimi Oratoris Magistri Johannis Russell, decretorum doctoris ac adtunc Ambassiatoris Edwardi Regis Anglie et Francie ad illustr. Principem Karolum ducem Burgundie super susceptione ordinis garterij,' &c., 4to.

3. ' The Recuyell of the Historyes of Troye, composed and drawen out of diverce bookes of latyn into Frensshe by Raoul le ffeure in the yere 1464, and drawen out of frensshe in to Englisshe by William Caxton at the commaundement of Margarete Duchess of Burgoyne, &c., whych sayd translacion and werke was begonne in Brugis in 1468 and ended in the holy cyte of Colen 19 Sept. 1471,' fol.

4. ' The Game and Playe of the Chesse, translated out of the French, fynysshid the last day of Marche, 1474,' fol.

5. A second edition of the same, fol. (with woodcuts).

6. ' A Boke of the hoole lyf of Jason' (1475), fol.

7. ' The Dictes and notable wyse Sayenges of the Phylosophers, transl. out of Frenshe by lord Antoyne Wydeville Erle Ryuyeres, cmpr. at Westmestre, 1477,' fol.

8. ' The Morale Prouerbes of Christyne (of Pisa),' fol. 1478.

9. ' The Book named Cordyale; or Memorare Novissima, which treateth of The foure last Things,' begun 1478, finished 1480, fol.

10. ' The Chronicles of Englond,' Westm., 1480, fol.

11. ' Description of Britayne,' 1480, fol.

12. ' The Mirrour of the World or thymage of the same,' 1481, fol.

13. ' The Historye of Reynart the Foxe,' 1481, fol.

14. ' The Boke of Tullius de Senectute, with Tullius de Amicitia, and the Declamacyon, which laboureth to shew wherein honour sholde reste,' 1481, fol.

15. ' Godefroy of Boloyne; or, the laste Siege and Conqueste of Jherusalem,' Westm., 1481, fol.

16. ' The Polycronycon,' 1482, fol.

17. ' The Pylgremage of the Sowle ; ' translated from the French, Westm., 1483, fol.

18. ' Liber Festivalis, or Directions for keeping Feasts all the Yere,' Westm., 1483, fol.

19. ' Quatuor Sermones ' (without date), fol.

20. ' Confessio Amantis, that is to saye in Englisshe, The Confessyon of the Louer, maad and compyled by Johan Gower, squyer,' Westm., 1483, fol.

21. ' The Golden Legende,' Westm., 1483, fol.

22. Another edition of ' The Legende,' sm. folio.

23. A third, ' fin. at Westmestre,' 20th May, 1483, fol.

24. ' The Booke callid Cathon' (Magnus), translated from the French, 1483, fol.

25. ' Parvus Chato' (without printer's name or date, but in Caxton's type), folio.

26. ' The Knyght of the Toure,' translated from the French; Westm. (1484), fol.

27. ' The Subtyl Historyes and Fables of Esope,' translated from the French, 1484, fol.

28. ' The Book of the Ordre of Chyvalry, or Knyghthode,' translated from the French (assigned to 1484), fol.

29. ' The Book ryal ; or the Book for a Kyng,' 1484, fol.

30. ' A Book of the noble Historyes of Kynge Arthur and of certen of his Knyghtes, which book was reduced in to Englysshe by syr Thomas Malory Knyght,' 1485, fol.

31. 'The Lyf of Charles the Grete Kyng of Fraunce and Emperour of Rome,' 1485, fol.

32. Another edition of the same, 1485, fol.

33. 'Thystorye of the noble ryght valyaunt and worthy Knyghte Parys and of the fayr Vyenne, the doulphyns doughter of Vyennoys,' translated from the French, 1485, fol.

34. 'The Book of Good Maners,' 1486, fol.

35. 'The Doctrinal of Sapyence,' translated from the French, 1489, fol.

36. ' The Book of Fayttes of Armes and of Chyvalrye,' a translation from the first part of Vegetius de Re Militari, 1489, fol.

37. 'The Arte and Crafte to knowe well to dye,' translated from the French, 1490, fol.

38. 'The Boke of Eneydos, compyled by Vyrgyle,' translated from the French, 1490, fol.

39. ' The Talis of Cauntyrburye ' (no date), fol.

40. Another edition (without date or place), fol.

41. 'Infancia Salvatoris,' 4to.

42. 'The Boke of Consolacion of Philosophie, whiche that Boecius made for his comforte and consolacion ' (no date nor place), fol.

43. A collection of Chaucer's and Lydgate's Minor Poems, 4to.

44. 'The Book of Fame, made by Geffcrey Chaucer,' fol.

45. ' Troylus and Creseyde,' fol.

46. ' A Book for Travellers,' fol.

47. ' The Lyf of St. Katherin of Senis,' fol.

48. 'Speculum Vite Christi ; or the myrroure of the blessyd Lyf of Jhesu Criste,' fol.

49. 'Directorium Sacerdotum : sive Ordinale secundum Usum Sarum,' Westm., fol.

50. 'The Worke (or Court) of Sapience,' composed by John Lydgate, fol.

51. ' A Boke of divers Ghostly Maters,' Westm., fol.

52. ' The Curial made by Maystre Alain Charretier,' translated from the French, fol.

53. ' The Lyf of our Lady, made by Dan John Lydgate, monke of Burye,' fol.

54. ' The Lyf of Saynt Wenefryde, reduced into Englisshe,' fol.

55. ' A Lytel Tretise, intytuled or named The Lucidarye,' 4to.

56. ' Reverendissimi viri dni. Gulielmi Lyndewodi, LLD. et

epi Asaphensis constitutiones provinciales Ecclesiæ Anglicanæ,' 24mo.

57. ' The Hystorye of Kynge Blanchardyne and Queen Eglantyne his wife,' fol.

58. 'The Siege of the noble and invyncyble Cytee of Rhodes,' fol.

59. 'Statuta apud Westmonasterium edita, anno primo Regis Ricardi tercii,' fol.

60. 'Statutes' made in the 1st, 2nd, and 3rd Parliaments of Henry VII., folio. (The only fragment of this work known consists of two leaves.)

61. ' The Accidence' (mentioned in one of the sale catalogues of the library of T. Martin of Palgrave).

62. ' The Prouffytable Boke of mānes soule, called The Chastysing of Goddes Chyldren,' fol.

63. ' Horæ,' &c., 12mo, a fragment of eight pages, now at Oxford, in the library bequeathed to the Bodleian by the late F. Douce, Esq.

64. A fragment of a Ballad, preserved in a volume of scraps and ballads in the British Museum.

From the time of Caxton's press to that of Thomas Hacket, we have the enumeration of 2926 books in Dr. Dibdin's work. The ' Typographical Antiquities' of Ames and Herbert comes down to a later period. They recorded the names of three hundred and fifty printers in England and Scotland, or of foreign printers engaged in producing books for England, that flourished between 1474 and 1600. The same authors have recorded the titles (we have counted with sufficient accuracy to make the assertion) of nearly 10,000 distinct works printed amongst us during the same period. Many of these works, however, were only single sheets; but on the other hand, there are doubtless many not here registered. Dividing the total number of books printed during these 130 years, we find that the average number of distinct works produced each year was 75.

APPENDIX C.

To avoid encumbering the preceding pages with foot-notes upon particular passages, the author subjoins a list of the principal books which he has referred to, or consulted, in this imperfect sketch of the Life of the Father of English Printing :—

'Typographical Antiquities, or an Historical Account of the Origin and Progress of Printing in Great Britain and Ireland.' By Joseph Ames and William Herbert. 3 vols. 4to, 1785.
    The same. Now greatly enlarged, with copious notes. By the Rev. Thomas Frognall Dibdin. 4 vols. 4to, 1810.
    'Biographia Britannica.' By Andrew Kippis. Article, 'Caxton,' in vol. iii., 1784.
    'Life of William Caxton.' Treatise, Library of Useful Knowledge. 1828.
    ' A Treatise on Wood Engraving, Historical and Practical.' With illustrations engraved on wood, by John Jackson. 1839.
    ' A Concise History of the Origin and Progress of Printing.' 1770.
    'Introduction to the Literature of Europe.' By Henry Hallam. Vol. i., 1836.
    ' Philobiblion, a Treatise on the Love of Books.' By Richard de Bury. Translated by John B. Inglis. 1832.
    'History of English Poetry.' By Thomas Warton. 4 vols. 8vo, 1824.
    'The Canterbury Tales of Chaucer.' With an Essay on his Language and Versification, &c. By Thomas Tyrwhitt. 5 vols., 1830.
    'Specimens of the Early English Poets,' to which is prefixed an

'Historical Sketch of the Rise and Progress of the English Poetry and Language.' By George Ellis. 3 vols., 1811.

'Illustrations of the Lives and Writings of Gower and Chaucer.' By the Rev. Henry J. Todd. 1810.

'Three Early English Metrical Romances.' Edited by John Robson for the Camden Society. 1842.

'Reliques of Ancient English Poetry.' By Thomas Percy. 3 vols., 1794.

'Minstrelsy of the Scottish Border.' By Sir Walter Scott. 'Introductory Remarks on Popular Poetry.' 1833.

'Sir Thomas More, or Colloquies on the Progress and Prospects of Society.' By Robert Southey. 2 vols., 1831.

'Utopia.' Written in Latin by Sir Thomas More. Translated by Ralph Robinson. A new edition, by the Rev. T. F. Dibdin. 2 vols., 1808.

'The History of London.' By Thomas Maitland. 2 vols. folio, 1756.

'The New Chronicles of England and France.' By Robert Fabyan. Edited by Sir Henry Ellis. 2 vols. 4to, 1811.

'The History of the Twelve Great Livery Companies of London.' By William Herbert. 2 vols. 8vo, 1834.

'Survey of the Cities of London and Westminster.' By John Stow. Augmented by John Strype. 2 vols. fol., 1720.

'Sir John Froissart's Chronicles.' Translated by Lord Berners. 2 vols. 4to, 1812.

'Memoirs of Philip de Comines.' Translated by Mr. Uvedale. 2 vols. 8vo. 1723.

'Paston Letters. Original Letters, written during the Reigns of Henry VI., Edward IV., and Richard III.' By Sir John Fenn. A new edition, by A. Ramsay. 2 vols., 1840.

'Histoire des Ducs de Bourgogne.' Par M. de Barante. 10 vols. 8vo, 1836.

'Statutes of the Realm.' From original records and authentic manuscripts. Vol. ii., 1816.

'Memoirs of Wool,' &c. By John Smith. 2 vols., 1747.

'Extracts from the Issue Rolls of the Exchequer, Henry III. to Henry VI.' 1837.

'Historie of the Arrivall of Edward IV.' Edited by John Bruce for the Camden Society. 1838.

'Wardrobe Accounts of Edward the Fourth.' By Nicholas
Harris Nicolas. 1830.

'Monasticon Anglicanum.' By Sir William Dugdale. Edition of
1817.

'Retrospective Review.' Vol. xv., Article, 'The Knight of the
Tower's Advice to his Daughters.'

www.ingramcontent.com/pod-product-compliance
Lightning Source LLC
Chambersburg PA
CBHW030902050726
47500CB00009B/985